TABOR EVANS

LONGARM

AND THE MISSING MARSHAL

JOVE BOOKS, NEW YORK

P9-CNI-054

THE BERKLEY PUBLISHING GROUP
Published by the Penguin Group
Penguin Group (USA) Inc.
375 Hudson Street, New York, New York 10014, USA
Penguin Group (Canada), 90 Eglinton Avenue East, Suite 700, Toronto, Ontario M4P 2Y3, Canada
(a division of Pearson Penguin Canada Inc.)
Penguin Books Ltd., 80 Strand, London WC2R 0RL, England
Penguin Group Ireland, 25 St. Stephen's Green, Dublin 2, Ireland (a division of Penguin Books Ltd.)
Penguin Group (Australia), 250 Camberwell Road, Camberwell, Victoria 3124, Australia
(a division of Pearson Australia Group Pty. Ltd.)
Penguin Books India Pvt. Ltd., 11 Community Centre, Panchsheel Park, New Delhi—110 017, India
Penguin Group (NZ), Cnr. Airborne and Rosedale Roads, Albany, Auckland 1310, New Zealand
(a division of Pearson New Zealand Ltd,)
Penguin Books (South Africa) (Pty.) Ltd., 24 Sturdee Avenue, Rosebank, Johannesburg 2196,
South Africa

Penguin Books Ltd., Registered Offices: 80 Strand, London WC2R 0RL, England

This is a work of fiction. Names, characters, places, and incidents either are the product of the author's imagination or are used fictitiously, and any resemblance to actual persons, living or dead, business establishments, events, or locales is entirely coincidental.

LONGARM AND THE MISSING MARSHAL

A Jove Book / published by arrangement with the author

PRINTING HISTORY
Jove edition / October 2006

Copyright © 2006 by The Berkley Publishing Group.

ISBN: 0-515-14208-5

JOVE®
Jove Books are published by The Berkley Publishing Group,
a division of Penguin Group (USA) Inc.,
375 Hudson Street, New York, New York 10014.
JOVE is a registered trademark of Penguin Group (USA) Inc.
The "J" design is a trademark belonging to Penguin Group (USA) Inc.

PRINTED IN THE UNITED STATES OF AMERICA

10 9 8 7 6 5 4 3 2 1

Caught in the Act

There was blood all over the place and people were screaming like crazy. Longarm shouted for them to settle down and try to be calm, but no one could hear his voice, so he marched on through the carnage. When he came to the platform between the cars, he peered out and saw a man on horseback who was being handed canvas sacks of money and jewelry by a man on foot.

"Hey!" Longarm yelled.

The man on the horse twisted around in his saddle and saw Longarm, who had holstered his gun and was now cocking both hammers of the shotgun. The other man, who had been handing up the bounty, froze in disbelief and then went for his six-gun . . .

DON'T MISS THESE
ALL-ACTION WESTERN SERIES
FROM THE BERKLEY PUBLISHING GROUP

THE GUNSMITH by J. R. Roberts
Clint Adams was a legend among lawmen, outlaws, and ladies. They called him . . . the Gunsmith.

LONGARM by Tabor Evans
The popular long-running series about Deputy U.S. Marshal Long—his life, his loves, his fight for justice.

SLOCUM by Jake Logan
Today's longest-running action Western. John Slocum rides a deadly trail of hot blood and cold steel.

BUSHWHACKERS by B. J. Lanagan
An action-packed series by the creators of Longarm! The rousing adventures of the most brutal gang of cutthroats ever assembled—Quantrill's Raiders.

DIAMONDBACK by Guy Brewer
Dex Yancey is Diamondback, a Southern gentleman turned con man when his brother cheats him out of the family fortune. Ladies love him. Gamblers hate him. But nobody pulls one over on Dex . . .

WILDGUN by Jack Hanson
The blazing adventures of mountain man Will Barlow—from the creators of Longarm!

TEXAS TRACKER by Tom Calhoun
Meet J.T. Law: the most relentless—and dangerous—man-hunter in all Texas. Where sheriffs and posses fail, he's the best man to bring in the most vicious outlaws—for a price.

Chapter 1

United States Deputy Marshal Custis Long was not in a particularly good mood on Monday morning when he went to work at the United States Federal Building located beside the Denver Mint. He had a woman problem *again*, specifically a woman named Molly Malloy who had managed to sweet-talk him into giving her a key to his apartment. Longarm had thought the key was to be used only occasionally for a tryst, but Molly had practically moved in lock, stock, and barrel.

It wasn't that Miss Malloy was a bad person, and she certainly was a handsome young woman, but Longarm was accustomed to living a bachelor life and sharing his apartment with his orange-striped alley cat and generally being free to come and go as he pleased. But that had all changed just over the weekend when Molly had had most of her furniture moved directly upstairs into Longarm's cramped apartment while he was playing almost nonstop poker with some friends.

He'd tried to kick Molly out of his humble apartment in a nice, reasonable manner, but Molly was a stubborn woman and not one given to hints or even gentle nudges.

1

"I'll have to take an afternoon off when she is at work and move everything back downstairs to her apartment," he muttered with irritation because it would be hard physically and an embarrassment for them both. Hell, the whole apartment building would be laughing their butts off over this misunderstanding. Even worse was when Molly found out that she had been dispossessed, because she would turn into a screaming witch whose cursing could be heard all the way to Cheyenne.

"Good morning, Marshal Long," a pretty young secretary called as Longarm marched into the Federal Building. "Did you have a nice weekend?"

Longarm knew that the girl, whose name he could never quite remember, was smitten with him, and he had made a mental note to invite her out to dinner and see if she was as bold and frisky as she always appeared. But that would sure have to wait until he got Molly to leave his apartment.

"Morning," Longarm said, trying to muster up a smile at the pretty thing, but barely managing as he hurried on down the hallway.

"Mr. Vail wants to see you in his office right away!" the girl called after him. "He said it is very urgent."

Longarm groaned because "urgent" usually meant that he was being offered an emergency assignment in some gawd-awful part of the West. Well, maybe the best thing that could happen was for him to leave town . . . as soon as he got Molly Malloy out of his place and then had the lock to his apartment door changed.

Longarm went to his desk and removed his coat because the office was warm and stuffy. He straightened his string tie and hung his snuff-brown Stetson on an ancient hat rack.

"Mornin', Custis," a beefy deputy marshal named Holcomb said, looking more chipper than a man should look on a workday Monday morning. "Say, you look a little worn out this morning, old buddy. What's the matter, did your latest saloon conquest screw the last of your brains out last night?"

"Shut up," Longarm growled.

"Ahh," Holcomb said with a cheerful grin. "You've just got to learn to ease up and quit trying to bed every woman in town. You're not a kid anymore, Custis. A man your age needs to know his physical limitations . . . something you haven't yet done."

Longarm was in no mood for banter, and he didn't particularly like Holcomb, so he snapped, "Yeah, physical limitations. I'm glad you've learned yours."

Holcomb frowned. "And they are?"

"Your pecker is tiny and thinner than a matchstick."

Holcomb was very sensitive about his physical attributes, which were all on the smallish side except for his bald head, which was abnormally large and made him look like a gnome. "My pecker is plenty long!"

"My guess is that you have to tie a cord to it so you can find it to pee," Longarm said, starting to smile.

"Bullshit!"

"Go on and unbutton your pants and show me that there isn't a cord tied to it," Longarm taunted, feeling better for the first time that morning. "I dare you."

Holcomb's entire head reddened and he stammered with indignation. "Well, maybe I just will!"

"No, you won't," Longarm said, turning to leave for his boss's office. "Because then it would be clear that your pecker is as withered as a little weed."

Holcomb wasn't in a jolly mood anymore, which

3

suited Longarm just fine as he walked down the hall hearing the man yelling at him. That made Longarm smile with quiet satisfaction because Deputy Holcomb wasn't fit to wear a lawman's badge. He was afraid to go out on dangerous assignments, and Longarm knew from firsthand experience that he couldn't ride or shoot a gun for sour owl shit.

Marshal Billy Vail's pendulum clock was striking half past nine o'clock when Longarm sauntered into his supervisor's office. He knew he was late . . . but this thing with Molly had lasted most of the night and he was exhausted and not about to apologize for his usual Monday morning tardiness.

"Ah, saints be praised because the famous Marshal Custis Long has arrived at last!" Billy said, his voice dripping with sarcasm. "And I can see by your face that you've had a very fun-filled weekend . . . again."

"Cut the crap, Billy," Longarm said with a yawn.

"Was that Deputy Holcomb I just heard screaming at you down the hallway?"

"Maybe."

"You really shouldn't bait the fella and get him so upset," Billy warned, leaning forward in his office chair and looking concerned. "Holcomb is a sworn officer of the law and he deserves at least some respect."

"Not from me he doesn't."

"He looks up to you," Billy said. "All the deputies I have on staff look up to you. So when you mistreat and insult poor Holcomb, he takes it very personally."

"I take him very personally," Longarm growled. "Because he can't muster up the gumption and ability to do his job, I get all the bad assignments while he sits on his little

4

butt and doodles or reads dime novels about Wild Bill Hickok or Buffalo Bill. My Gawd, why did you ever hire someone like that?"

"I had no choice," Billy confessed. "As usual, it was all politics. Holcomb's family is very influential at the mayor's office and we needed a local liaison. Someone who can grease the city's political wheels and help us do our jobs better in this town. Need I remind you that Holcomb was born and raised in Denver and that his family knows everyone who is anyone?"

"No."

"And Holcomb is very good at assisting this office in getting cooperation from the city police. So he earns his pay just like you do . . . only from a desk chair."

"Holcomb is just an ass-kisser who should never have been given a badge and a gun. One of these days he might try to arrest someone with his pistol, and then they will shove it up his backside and pull the trigger. When that happens, you are going to be in a lot of deep shit, Billy. It's going to backfire on you like you wouldn't believe."

"Ah," Billy said dismissively, "let's not talk about Deputy Holcomb anymore. I have far more pressing and important things to discuss."

"Such as?"

"Have you heard of Major Fremont P. Gumm?"

"Of course," Longarm said. "He was one of the most promising and fastest-rising military men in the entire Union Army until a Confederate sniper shot him in the head."

"That's right. It was a tragedy."

"I suppose that depends on your point of view, Billy."

"Ah yes, you are from By-Gawd West Virginia. But that

aside, Major Gumm was a gallant soldiers and he was fearless. His loss was felt by everyone right up to and including Ulysses S. Grant."

"I'm sure you're correct," Longarm said, taking a chair. "But that's history and I was told that we have an emergency. So why don't you get to the point?"

"I *am* getting to the point. What I have to tell you relates directly to the great Major Gumm."

"I am on the edge of my chair waiting in anticipation to hear this," Longarm said, trying to stifle a yawn.

Billy frowned. "You really must have had a bad weekend. What happened, some woman screw your brains out last night and wanted more than you could finally give her?"

"Let's stick to the subject," Longarm said. "Tell me why I need to hear about Major Fremont P. Gumm this Monday morning."

"You need to hear about him because of his son . . . and his son's fiancée."

Longarm frowned, not understanding.

"Did you know," Billy said, leaning on his desk with his elbows, "that Major Gumm's only son, Bradford G. Gumm, went west in search of his own fame and fortune and ended up being deputized as a United States marshal?"

"No," Longarm said with real disbelief.

"Well, it's true. I didn't know it myself until Friday afternoon and when I tried to catch and tell you . . . you had already left for the weekend."

"I had some pressing business," Longarm explained.

"I'm sure you did. Pressing something soft and wet."

"Gumm," Longarm snapped.

"Ah, yes, young, adventurous, rich, and handsome Bradford G. Gumm, the spitting image of his great war hero father. The heartthrob of Washington, D.C., society women. The most prized bachelor in the East."

"And?" Longarm asked.

Billy steepled his chubby fingers and said, "And Bradford went west in a blaze of glory and ended up . . . missing."

Longarm had started to lean forward in his chair, but now he sat back abruptly. "What do you mean, 'missing'?"

"He has vanished in Arizona. Near Pine Valley, Arizona, to be more specific. Custis, have you ever been to Pine Valley?"

"Can't say I have."

"Well, I haven't either," Billy said. "But I'm told it is up on the Mogollon Rim, which is high country in the eastern part of the territory. Great cattle-raising country, but unfortunately also great sheep-raising country."

"Billy, would you please just get to the point of all this?" Longarm said with exasperation.

"The point is that young Bradford G. Gumm went west in search of his own fame and he knew that he needed to be thrust into something that was epic . . . and newsworthy. So he chose to inject himself into one of the worst, bloodiest, and longest-lasting range wars on the entire frontier."

"A sheep-against-cattle war," Longarm said, finally getting the picture.

"Exactly. I don't know much about this long-running feud, but over the weekend I have made some inquiries and I've discovered that it is very bad. Even worse than what happened in Montana's Chilton Valley War."

"That war took the lives of no less than twenty sheep men and cattlemen," Longarm said. "I've been there and there are two separate cemeteries in Chilton Valley. Both have been looted and desecrated by one faction or the other's surviving womenfolk. All men of fighting age in Chilton Valley, of course, have been killed off."

"A terrible thing," Billy said, shaking his head.

"And this range war in Arizona is even worse?" Longarm asked in obvious disbelief.

"So I'm told. No one has an exact count, but the death toll is said to be over thirty men and even a few women. It's a terrible feud that no one believes will ever end until there is no one left old enough to hold a gun or a rifle."

"And into this hell went our young Eastern fame-seeking Bradford G. Gumm," Longarm said darkly.

"Yes, I'm afraid so. Bradford must be a complete fool. I do know that he is no coward and he's killed a rival in a duel. He is also reputed to be an expert marksman and very accomplished pugilist."

"Which means nothing when he is in the middle of a range war where men prefer to back-shoot their enemies or most anyone else who even appears to be taking one side of the feud against the other."

"Precisely so," Billy agreed. "And now I must tell you about a visitor that is about to arrive and meet with us."

"Let me guess. One of the other glory-hound Gumms?"

"Almost," Billy said with a thin smile. "And by that I mean that this is the *future* Miss Bradford G. Gumm."

"She's coming here?" Longarm asked.

"Oh, yes. And I have heard through the grapevine that she is a beauty, but also a man-eater. A real social climber who is every bit as ambitious and publicity-hungry as her missing Bradford."

Longarm moaned. "This gets worse by the moment. What is this woman coming here for?"

"She has arrived from the East with great fanfare and

publicity to learn the fate and whereabouts of her dear Bradford. The young woman insists that she will accompany you to Pine Valley, Arizona."

"No damned way!" Longarm cried, jumping to his feet. "I don't want any part of this range war . . . or this woman."

"I know that," Billy said, suddenly looking troubled. "But the fact of the matter is that we have no choice."

"What is this 'we' business!"

"Take it easy, Custis."

"I'm not going to Arizona and I'm damn sure not taking this woman."

Billy sighed with resignation. "Then I'll probably be fired from my job. I'll lose my pension, my home, and almost certainly my wife and children will become destitute. I will probably wind up putting a pistol to my head and ending my life within the next few months."

"Stop it, Billy! This isn't funny."

"I wish that it were," Billy said, his eyes turning bleak with dread, "but I'm not joking. I will be fired."

"Why!"

"Because that is the way it is going to happen," he said, suddenly looking old and sad. "It's all politics. If I fail to send someone to Pine Valley, Arizona, and they fail to find and recover Bradford, then the publicity will be relentless and unmerciful. I'll be asked to resign and when I refuse, I'll be fired."

Longarm stared into the eyes of his boss and friend and he saw that Billy was telling the unvarnished truth.

"If that is the way of it," Longarm heard himself say, "then I'll have no choice but to go."

"You have a choice. I don't even have to mention your name to this young woman. I could send someone else."

"There is no one else that would stand a chance of surviving a range war," Longarm reminded his boss. "We both know that."

"Yes, we do."

"Shit," Longarm muttered, wishing he'd not awakened this Monday morning.

"That aptly describes it," Billy agreed.

"So what time is this woman supposed to arrive?"

"Sometime late this afternoon."

Longarm glanced up at the big wall clock with its swinging pendulum. He felt as if he were being swung back and forth himself just as helplessly as the pendulum. "I'll be back early this afternoon. No later than four."

"Thanks," Billy said, unable to hide his immense relief. "You should go home and put on your best and cleanest suit. You forgot to shave again, and that would help. Get a haircut and return wearing a big, welcoming smile."

"I won't patronize or flatter this woman," Longarm said. "I'll let her come along with me, but I won't try to ingratiate myself to her."

"You must be on your best behavior. I expect you to behave as the gentleman that I know you to be," Billy told him. "This woman may not be nearly as bad as her bark. She might be very charming, in fact."

"I doubt that."

"Actually so do I," Billy said. "But will you please try to be nice to her and at least a little accommodating?"

"If I must."

"You must," Billy said. "And I'll try to make it up for you somehow when you return."

"*If* I return."

"You will," Billy said, "you always do. Now will you clean up a bit?"

"I'll spiffy up some," Longarm said, knowing he did

look rather careworn this morning. "But I won't be able to smile."

"All right. I'll smile enough for both of us."

Longarm shook his head. "I wouldn't have your job for anything, Billy."

"And I wouldn't have yours," Billy said truthfully.

Chapter 2

Longarm's apartment was only a few blocks from the Federal Building, and before he went there he stopped at the barbershop for a first-class haircut and a shave. Then he headed on back to his apartment intent on taking a long nap and preparing for the unwelcome challenge of meeting Bradford Gumm's obnoxious and publicity-seeking fiancée. He tried to remember if Billy Vail had even told him her name.

"Custis, what are you doing back here so early?" Molly Malloy said when he opened his door and found her reclining in his favorite easy chair with a cup of coffee in her hand.

"I was about to ask you the same thing," he said, closing the door behind him and hanging up his hat and coat. "How come you aren't working at the hat shop this morning?"

Molly was a red-haired Irish girl and extremely easy on the eyes. She boasted a peaches-and-cream complexion and an hourglass figure. Molly caused men everywhere to stop in their tracks and stare, but she wasn't a flirt and she wasn't easy. Rather, she was a very strong-willed young woman who had decided that Longarm was the man she wanted to marry someday.

"Oh, didn't I tell you that I quit that job?" Molly replied. "I'm going back to working at Clancy's Saloon. I can earn more in tips there in one night than I could make at the hat shop in a week. And it's a lot more fun."

"But you told me that you wanted a day job," Longarm said, removing his holster and gun and placing them on a piece of Molly's furniture. "And I recall you saying that you wanted to save up enough money to open your own millinery shop."

Molly shrugged. "Well, I would never be able to save much money working at the hat shop, and besides, Clancy gave me a big raise because he said I was very good for his business. I won't work at Clancy's too long. Maybe just another six months. One year, tops."

"Just remember that old Clancy wants more than you want to give," Longarm said. "He's crazy for you."

"Yeah," Molly replied without caring, "I know. Clancy asked me to marry him again today. That makes . . . twelve times . . . I think. That big lug really has the lust for me, but I'm *your* girl, Custis."

To show she meant what she said, Molly came over and wrapped her arms around Custis's neck, then kissed him wetly on the mouth. "You still love me?"

"Sure," Longarm said, "but . . ."

"No buts about it," Molly said, placing a finger over his lips. "And I'm sorry I didn't tell you that I was moving everything I own up here to your apartment."

"It's so crowded I can hardly move around, and my cat left because he hates the smell of your perfume."

"He'll be back when he gets hungry enough. And actually, Custis, I never really intended to do that, but once I started moving a few things, I just thought what the hell. Might as well move in completely."

"Yeah," Longarm said, glancing around an apartment so crowded with furniture and boxes that it was almost impossible to navigate. "But Molly, this just isn't going to work out. I can't live with so much clutter and confusion."

Molly Malloy was wearing a pink dress and nothing much else underneath. The woman disliked underclothing, and now she was rubbing her big breasts against his chest and nibbling on his earlobe.

"Honey," she whispered, "I'm really sorry about the misunderstanding we had this weekend. I'll get rid of some of our stuff so it won't be so cluttered. And, if you really want, I'll move out after a while."

Her tongue was wetting the inside of his ear and her breath was warm. Longarm could already feel his manhood rising. "Well," he hedged, hating himself for the weakness of his flesh, "I guess you don't have to hurry about it."

"I don't?" she cooed, hand sliding down to his crotch and then rubbing him in all the right places.

"No," he said, realizing that he was getting a huge hard-on. "I mean, I just learned that I'll have to rush off to Arizona."

Molly pushed back with her green eyes suddenly filled with disappointment. "Tomorrow?"

"I'm afraid so."

"Then we'd better make the best of today," she said, starting to unbutton his trousers. "Wouldn't you agree?"

Longarm gulped and his hand found the mounds of her magnificent breasts. "Well, that doesn't sound half bad," he said as her hand gently closed around his already throbbing rod.

She giggled. "Let's go to bed and see if we can make ourselves scream and shout. How about that, big boy?"

Longarm found himself nodding and then half-

15

dragging Molly over boxes and excess furniture as he rushed her to his bed. It was covered with her clothes and more boxes, but he swept them off with his arm and then threw her down on the mattress.

"I came home to get some sleep," he said weakly.

"Yeah, sure you did," Molly said as she started lifting her skirt to expose her long, bare legs. "Would you like it right now with our clothes on . . . or should I undress completely?"

Longarm knelt on the bed beside her. "Lift that dress up a little higher and let's get after it right now!"

Molly yanked her dress up so that it bunched around her narrow waist. She spread her silken thighs and gave him a little bump with her hips. "Come to your hard-lovin' Irish girl," she breathed. "Come and fill me with your big, sweet potato."

Longarm stared at the dark, glistening auburn-colored mound of her womanhood and momentarily tried to remind himself that he needed sleep and that he would just poke her this once before he closed his eyes and rested. But then he grinned, knowing that he would savage voluptuous Molly at least four times before four o'clock.

And why not? After all, he was being sent to Arizona to try to end a bloody range war and he had as company, instead of another lawman to help him stay alive . . . an Eastern socialite who from all accounts was a self-serving bitch.

Might as well get all the joy I can out of this world right here and now, Longarm happily decided as he drove his huge rod into Molly's hot honey hole.

Longarm and Molly just fit together like well-oiled machinery. Their thrusting and banging was in perfect unison and their climaxes were thundering affairs that ended up in shouts and screams. Other tenants in the apartment building heard their wild orgy of lovemaking and either cussed them in fits of rage or jealousy, or smiled in remembrance as the day wore on and the sweating, grasping, and thrusting couple upstairs gradually and finally wore down.

"Custis, darling? Custis, wake up. It's getting late and I've got to get dressed and head off to Clancy's Saloon."

Longarm awoke with a start. He couldn't have been sleeping more than an hour . . . but when he glanced out his window he saw that he'd been asleep for much longer.

"What time is it?" he asked groggily.

"It's five o'clock."

"Oh, damn!" he groaned. "I promised Billy that I'd be back no later than four."

"Well, everyone is late sometime," she said, leaning over and kissing him tenderly. "And we had a very good reason to be late. Actually, we had five reasons for being late . . . or was it six?"

Longarm had to chuckle. "I lost count, but I do know that all of them were good."

Molly got up and said, "I'm going down the hall to take a bath. We both smell like draft horses . . . or maybe draft horses that have been coupling all day."

Longarm sniffed. "Yeah, I see what you mean. Molly, do you mind if I take that bath first? I have to hurry."

"Well, so do I," she said, grabbing a bath towel and heading for the door. "You see, I promised Clancy I'd be at his place by six o'clock when it starts to get real busy. I'm sure you can understand that I can't be late on my first night back at the saloon."

Longarm knew that it was impossible to argue with this

Irish girl and that, if he tried, it might even escalate into a big battle, so he just nodded. "All right. I'll just take a basin bath here and hurry off to the office."

"Will I see you when I get off work early this morning?"

"I don't know," he told her. "You get off when?"

"About three in the morning. I could wake you up and we could have a lusty good-bye. One that you'll carry with you all the way to Arizona and back. One that will make you think twice about messing with another woman while you're away from me."

"We'll see," Longarm said. "I think we pretty much did all the good-byin' we can stand."

Molly bent over and kissed the head of his red and sore root. "We'll grease up better in the morning and you'll be as good as new."

"Molly," he said in absolute amazement, "you're a walking physical wonder."

"And so are you, big boy. See you about three o'clock this morning."

"Okay."

When she was gone, Longarm poured water out of a porcelain pitcher and found a washcloth. He washed his tender privates and then he looked at himself in the mirror. Longarm wasn't pleased with the face that reflected back at him. There were dark circles under his eyes and he looked older than his actual years.

"I've got to get away from that woman before she screws the life outa me," he muttered to himself. "But there's no sense in insisting that she leave now. I'll talk to her again about it when I return from Arizona."

Longarm finished his little cleanup and splashed a palm full of cologne on his body trying to dampen a pervasive smell of heavy sex. Then he found clean underwear, his best clean shirt, and his newest tailored suit. It was brown, like his polished boots and expensive felt hat. When he finished dressing, he put on a tie and briefly admired his shaved face, trying to ignore the big hickeys that Molly had implanted on both sides of his throat while carried away in her deepest throes of passion. To hide the hickeys, he hiked up his collar and buttoned it tight.

Some of the damage still peeked over his collar, but that couldn't be helped at this late hour. Besides, this high-society woman would no doubt think they were simply razor burns.

"Billy is going to be furious if she's there already," he said to himself as he strapped on his gun and set his Stetson just right on top of his barbered hair. "I hope the damned train she arrived on had a wreck."

But Longarm knew that he didn't really mean that . . . or did he?

Chapter 3

"Oh, dear gracious me, Marshal Long," the pretty secretary in the Federal Building fretted, "I'm afraid that you're really going to catch it when you go up to Mr. Vail's office."

"Yeah, I guess I'm late again, huh?"

"Very. And that rich woman is furious!"

Longarm squared his broad shoulders. He was six-feet-four, and with his Stetson adding about two more inches, he was an extremely imposing figure in any group. But right now he was feeling a bit small, and had the strongest urge just to turn around and march back out of the building. But he couldn't do that because his boss and friend's job was on the line.

"Because I'm late?"

"I suppose," the secretary said. "And I have to say that Mr. Vail has been down here three times in the last hour asking me if anyone has seen you in the building."

"Might as well go up there and face the music," Longarm said. "Can't be worse than getting shot."

"I should hope not."

Longarm took a deep breath and headed upstairs as he smoothed his suit and shirt. He wished he'd had time to bathe, but he'd have to make do with all the cologne he'd splashed on himself.

"So there you are!" Billy cried, nearly leaping over his desk when Longarm appeared in the doorway. "Where the . . . heck have you been? We've been waiting here for you for nearly *two hours.*"

"I had some . . . uh . . . unexpected complications."

Billy was glowering at him, but Longarm didn't notice as he turned to face the woman from Washington, D.C., the fiancée of Bradford G. Gumm. She would have been beautiful had it not been for the fury that possessed her face. Dark eyes flashing with anger, mouth pressed into a thin, pale line, jaw hard and uncompromising. She was tall for a woman, and her arms were folded across what appeared to be a very attractive bosom. Diamonds and emeralds glittered on her fingers and her fingernails were long, red, and sharp.

Before the Eastern high-society woman could light into Longarm, Billy cleared his voice loudly and proclaimed, "Miss Julia Konrad, this is my very *best* Deputy Marshal, Custis Long . . . better known as Longarm among us professionals. And he has eagerly agreed to accompany you to Arizona in search of—"

"I hate being made to wait!" Julia shouted, cutting Billy off. "Marshal Long, who in God's name do you think you are making me stand around cooling my heels after I've come so far to find my dear Bradford? Do you know that I know people who could have you and your boss fired!"

Longarm had expected anger, but this was way over the top. Momentarily stunned by her vehemence, he was at a loss for words.

Billy, fortunately, came to his rescue. "Miss Konrad,

22

I'm sure that Deputy Marshal Long has a very good reason for his tardiness. But that aside, perhaps—"

"Let's hear it," Julia snapped. "And your reason had better be deathbed serious."

Longarm had regained his composure, and now he felt both anger and an instant dislike for this imperious woman. "To tell you the truth, Miss Konrad, the reason I am late is personal and none of your business."

For a moment it appeared that Julia Konrad might spring at Longarm and rake him with those long red fingernails. Go straight for his eyes and try to claw them out of their sockets. She turned pale and shook like she had the palsy and when she spoke, Julia's voice was like crunching glass.

She raised her hand and pointed a shaky finger at him yelling, "Get out of my sight, you big, rude buffoon!"

If there was one thing Longarm hated, it was taking orders. And when those orders were given in such a mean spirit, he was doubly insulted and annoyed.

Folding his own arms across his chest, Longarm said, "I'm not going anywhere until I feel like it, Miss Konrad. And I sure don't appreciate being insulted."

"You *deserve* to be insulted! You kept me waiting here!"

"Two hours isn't worth getting all sweated up over," Longarm said. "And it doesn't give you the right to treat me like a slave or subhuman being. I won't stand for that."

"You what?" she cried.

"I won't stand being insulted and yelled at," Longarm said, arms still folded and jaw just as clenched as hers. "And for all I care, you can go not only to Arizona on your own, but also straight to hell."

Billy threw up his hands and moaned as if he'd been

punched in his considerable gut. He staggered and collapsed back in his leather desk chair and covered his round face with his hands as if he could block out this ongoing nightmare.

"Assign me another lawman," Julia Konrad ordered, turning on Billy. "I wouldn't even go across the street with this obnoxious, incompetent moron who works for you."

Billy dropped his hands from his face and shook his head. "Miss Konrad, I am very sorry, but there isn't a man on my force that I would even think about sending into something as bad as the range war that is going on in Pine Valley, Arizona. If I sent Holcomb or someone else, they'd not only get themselves killed, but you as well."

Julia Konrad cried out in disbelief, "Surely you must be jesting! Surely thee is someone that you can assign to me that is worthy of being a United States marshall!"

"Good men are real hard to find," Billy said, straightening up in his chair and finally exhibiting a bit of backbone. "And Custis Long, while he may have his faults . . . is brave, resourceful, and absolutely the finest officer I have ever had the pleasure of commanding."

Longarm had never been praised so highly by Billy, and now he felt like he wanted to go over to his supervisor and give him a big hug. And he probably would have done it if the impossibly arrogant Miss Julia Konrad hadn't been standing directly between them.

Julia took a deep breath and studied Longarm from his polished brown boots to the top of his Stetson hat. She unfolded her arms and took several deep breaths before she said, "All right, Marshal Long, offer your sincerest apology and I'll find it in my heart to forgive you for making me wait."

Longarm wasn't good at apologies. In fact, he could

count on one hand the number of times he'd had to swallow his pride and make an apology. And right now he wasn't of a mind to apologize even a bit . . . except that he could see the pleading in Billy Vail's eyes. It was clear that a concession had to be made or Billy was going to suffer the consequences.

Longarm cleared his throat. "I'm sorry I kept you waiting."

Billy exhaled so loudly that they both glanced at him. Then Julia looked back at Longarm and snapped, "I accept your apology, but you must *never* let that happen again."

Longarm clamped his jaw and bit back an uncomplimentary response.

"Now," Julia Konrad said with a look of triumph on her lovely face, "tell me the reason for your tardiness, Marshal Long."

Longarm wasn't taking any more guff from this woman and he was no longer going to accommodate her obviously inflated ego. "Like I told you, it was personal."

"Like a death in the family?" she asked almost hopefully.

"Something like that," Longarm lied.

But then her eyes narrowed and she asked, "Or a woman you couldn't bear to leave?"

Longarm's jaw dropped with surprise. "What would make you think that?"

"The hickey on your neck. Two hickeys, actually. And there are probably a lot more under that collar. How disgusting!"

Longarm felt his face turn hot. Damn, this woman didn't miss a whole hell of a lot.

"Well, ma'am, I . . ."

"You must be very much in love to have made such a

blunder . . . one that could have cost both yourself and Mr. Vail his job."

Suddenly and entirely without warning, her voice cracked with emotion. "I too am deeply in love, Marshal Long. But unlike yourself, I no longer can share the sweet embrace of my beloved, Bradford. And so that is why I must swallow my own pride at this moment and say that I will forgive you your rudeness in the name of your love. And I fervently request that you help me find my brave and darling Bradford."

Longarm found himself nodding because it was clear that these words had come from what little heart Julia Konrad possessed. It made him feel ashamed of himself for keeping her waiting and for taking such a hard line in the face of her fire. "All right, Miss Konrad," he heard himself saying. "Let's just pretend that we got off on the right foot here. You try to treat me almost as an equal and I'll try to be on time in the future and help you find your fiancé."

"Fair enough," Julia said. She was wearing white gloves and she stuck out her right hand, palm up. Longarm didn't think a man was supposed to kiss a gloved hand, and he wasn't in the habit of kissing a bare hand, either. So he grabbed her glove and shook it firmly.

Julia smiled and it was radiant. It was like she had transformed from a witch into a wonder. "Marshal Long, I would like us to leave for the Arizona Territory at once."

"There is a train out this evening," he heard himself say. "If we stop jawing and get to moving, we could catch it."

"Then by all means let's do that," Julia said, suddenly all business. "How long will it take to get to Pine Valley?"

"If we bust our . . . humps, ma'am, we can probably do it in ten days . . . maybe closer to a week."

"Then let's 'bust our humps,' Marshal Long. I am sick

at heart with the thought of my Bradford perhaps hurt or in some way restrained from contacting me."

"He could be dead," Longarm said, regretting the words the very instant they left his mouth even though that was a very strong possibility. "But then again he might be just fine."

"I don't think he is either," she told him, eyes growing moist with tears. "If he were fine, my gallant Bradford would have sent me a telegram."

"There probably isn't a telegraph line out of Pine Valley."

"Then a letter," she said, pushing on. "And if Bradford was dead, I would have heard about it, surely."

Longarm decided not to tell this woman that she had an Eastern mentality. That people died all the time on the frontier and their bodies were never found . . . maybe only their bones years later. No, there was no sense in telling Miss Julia Konrad the grim truth that it was quite likely that her foolish fiancé was already dead.

"We will meet at the train station, then?"

He nodded and extracted his pocket watch. It was an Ingersoll watch and one end of the gold chain was attached to a solid-brass, twin-barreled derringer. It was a .44-caliber and it had saved his life on more than one desperate occasion.

"Our Denver and Rio Grande will be leaving for Pueblo in exactly sixty-five minutes. From there we'll take the Santa Fe and after that a stagecoach, buckboard, or . . . if forced to it, horses. Can you ride a horse, Miss Konrad? And are you willing and ready to suffer some hardships in order to get to Pine Valley?"

"I am," she promised. "You may think me spoiled and pampered . . . and I am. But I am also tough and determined. When I make my mind up about something, I am an unstoppable force."

"Ma'am," Longarm said, "I believe that. I really do. But there is one thing I would strongly recommend you do before we board that train."

"And that is?"

"Get rid of all that jewelry. It'll attract thieves and cut-throats like flies to . . . to sugar water. And go to the mercantile and buy yourself some rough outdoor outfits. Not too many because we'll have to travel light and fast. But some good hiking boots and a hat are a must. I'll bring everything else we need."

"I am not accustomed to not wearing jewelry." She flashed her diamond engagement ring, which must have been at least three carats. "And I won't leave this behind. I will wear it to my grave."

Longarm saw no reason to point out that a ring worth that much money could cause her to go to an early grave. "Well, then," he said, "put the other jewels in a local bank vault and turn that ring around when we're among rough men. We'll have enough of a challenge to get to Arizona without having to deal with men who would slit your throat for ten dollars, much less ten thousand dollars."

"I'm sure Bradford paid far more than ten thousand for my engagement ring," she said icily. "But your point is well taken and I will do as you suggest."

"Good. Oh, and buy a rain slicker, too."

She frowned. "Do you expect we'll hit some bad weather?"

"I not only expect it, I'll guarantee it," Longarm told her.

"I suppose that must be endured, then." Julia Konrad managed a smile, and then she was hurrying out the door to make her preparations for the long and difficult journey that they both faced.

"Well," Billy said, slumping in his chair as though he

had run a mile at altitude, "I thought for a few minutes we were both cooked. That our careers were over and that we would soon be holding tin cups and begging for small coins on the streets."

"Ah," Longarm said with a chuckle, "you know that we'd have done all right even it Miss Konrad had gotten us sacked. Do you think she really could have done that?"

"Unquestionably," Billy assured him. "And for God's sakes, please try to be nice to her and keep her from getting hurt or killed. I won't sleep well at all until this whole miserable affair has been satisfactorily settled and all three of you return safe and sound."

"I'll do my best, Billy, but the woman is going to be like a millstone around my neck and that I don't need."

"I know. I know."

Longarm replaced his watch in his vest pocket. "I'm glad that you understand what we're up against in a range war. And taking an outspoken and hotheaded woman like that into the feud is just asking for failure and maybe even death."

"Custis," Billy said, his voice shaking with emotion. "If you somehow find this Bradford and bring him and Miss Konrad back alive, I will do *anything* you ask relative to your job. Anything!"

"How about a month of paid vacation and a twenty-dollar-a-month raise?"

Billy didn't even hesitate. "As good as done. I swear it."

Longarm was pleased. The best and only time to wring a concession from his boss was when the man's back was pressed tight against the wall.

"I'd like to have that promise in writing," Longarm said. "No offense, but I'd feel better if it was on paper."

"Don't push me."

Longarm knew from the man's tone of voice that he wasn't going to write anything down. "All right. I have to hurry back to my apartment and—"

"No!"

Longarm was surprised by this outburst. "Why not?"

"Do you really need to ask?" Billy demanded. "Remember that you left this office only this morning promising to return by four o'clock. I *know* what happened in your apartment this afternoon while I was here with Miss Konrad sweating bullets of blood. The truth is that you . . . you have no control over your physical urges, Custis. And I forbid you to return to that woman for one more good-bye."

Longarm could have told Billy that Molly was working at her saloon job, but chose otherwise. "I need to have luggage and extra clothes for the journey, Billy."

"You can buy everything you need for this trip on the way to Arizona. I'll get you enough travel money right now before you leave this building."

"You will?"

"Yes."

There was one more thing that Billy needed to be reminded of, and so Longarm said, "Miss Konrad will, of course, be traveling first class and not coach."

"True," Billy said, already sensing where this was leading.

"And if I am to protect her, I'd better be close at hand. Right?"

"I . . . I suppose."

"Then I'll need enough money to travel first class going and coming," Longarm said with an expansive smile.

"Dammit," Billy groused, "this is getting expensive."

"Not as expensive as us losing our jobs because I wasn't

nearby to protect the lady every minute of the night and the day."

Billy reluctantly nodded. "All right. You'll go first class."

"Both ways?"

"Yes, dammit, *both ways*."

"And, Billy, of course you do understand that Miss Konrad will also insist on dining in fine places. No greasy joints or hash houses. Steak and wine, that's how I read her. And no lady can be expected to dine alone."

"Custis, dammit, you're really starting to piss me off!"

Longarm grinned because he sure liked to travel first class all the way. Also, he knew that he had pushed his boss quite far enough.

Chapter 4

Miss Julia Konrad was pacing back and forth in front of the train while its whistle let out shrill blasts and its conductor was shouting "All aboard!"

Longarm was running hard down the long wooden loading platform with two big canvas bags filled with travel supplies, a Winchester rifle, blankets, canteens, and plenty of extra ammunition. He supposed he could have bought these things en route to Arizona, but he was sure that he'd saved a lot of money in Denver.

"Dammit!" Julie screamed furiously as the train started to roll. "You did it to me again!"

"Sorry, ma'am! Jump on board and I'll be right behind you."

It was fortunate the train was barely rolling because the woman was wearing high heels and a long dress. But she proved herself very athletic by grabbing a support bar and leaping onto the coach platform. Longarm caught a glimpse of her long, shapely legs almost up to her knees and what he saw was very attractive. He tossed his canvas bags up onto the train and jumped in beside Julia, who was so angry that she grabbed him by his lapels and tried to shake him like a terrier might a rat.

"What is the matter with you!" she demanded. "Can't you be on time for anything! Did you really have to bed your woman one more time . . . or what!"

Longarm was badly winded. He'd run from a hired carriage nearly two hundred yards away carrying the heavy satchels, and now it took him a few moments to catch enough breath to speak.

"Sorry, but I had a lot of stuff to collect for us. What I bought would have cost twice as much in the small towns. I was just trying to save the government money, that's all."

"I don't care about the government! If you need extra money for this trip, ask me for it. Do you understand?"

He removed his handkerchief from his pants and mopped his face free of sweat. "Yeah, lady, I understand. Now let's get you to your compartment so that I can have a drink and relax . . . maybe even get some shut-eye on the way down to Pueblo."

She balled her fists in his face and said, "If I didn't need you so bad on this miserable mission, I'd give you *two* shut-eyes! Or they'd be better described as shiners."

"Hmm, got a violent streak along with a violent temper, I see."

Julia said something unladylike that Longarm couldn't quite pick up because of the banging and clanking of the train as it gathered speed heading south out of Denver. He decided it was just as well.

Their southbound journey over Raton Pass and then later connecting with the Atchison, Topeka, and Santa Fe Railroad was a much-needed rest for Longarm. He mostly slept, met Miss Konrad in the superbly outfitted first-class

34

dining car, and then spent his time gazing out the window as the West rolled past.

In New Mexico they hit a cow. The very same afternoon the train was halted for six hours because a train trestle had been partially burned, probably by the Apache or maybe the Navajo, who did not appreciate the white man crossing their arid homeland. There were several construction crewmen on board the train and extra timbers and tools to fix the trestle, but no sign of Indians. And perhaps it hadn't been Indians at all, for there were many whites who had real or perceived grudges against the powerful Western railroads and delighted in causing them grief by destroying tracks and trestles.

For Longarm the delays did not matter. A few hours lost here or there were unimportant to him. Not so for Miss Konrad, however. Every moment delayed was a moment of lingering agony for the poor woman. She was, Longarm knew, driven to recover her long-lost fiancé and desperately worried about Bradford G. Gumm's health and welfare.

Longarm thought that was admirable. Julia Konrad was spoiled, haughty, and far too self-important, but the fact that she loved . . . really loved . . . Bradford Gumm was to her credit.

"What's he like?" Longarm asked as the train rolled across northern New Mexico heading for the eastern border of Arizona, the red-rock and high mesa country of the Hopi and the Navajo. They were sipping wine after having had a sumptuous dinner served with silver, crystal, and chinaware.

"You mean dear Bradford?"

"Yes."

Julia was in a better than usual mood because Longarm had told her that they would be arriving in the old railroad and logging town of Flagstaff in less than twenty-four hours. And from there they would try to catch a stagecoach south into the Mogollon Rim country and eventually reach Pine Valley, probably making the last stage on horseback.

"Hmm," she mused, mouth faintly smiling as she took another sip of an excellent cabernet. "That's not an easy question to answer. You have, of course, heard of Bradford's late father?"

"Of course," Longarm said. "Major Fremont G. Gumm was fearless as well as brilliant. He is still talked about in the North and some say he would have been even greater than Grant . . . had he survived the war. That he would have one day been the President of the United States."

"Undoubtedly," Julia said, gazing out the window at a dry and parched landscape. "Bradford, of course, was just a young boy when news came that his father had fallen on the battlefield. And although the senior Gumm was not an affectionate man to his only son, he was a great presence and young Bradford was in awe of him. So, when his father died, it was quite a blow. And Bradford's mother, who was always quite fragile, completely went to pieces. She had a total mental breakdown and soon had to be placed in an insane asylum where she died."

Longarm had known nothing of this. "So who raised Bradford from that point?"

"His grandmother, a doting old fool."

Longarm was surprised by this harsh assessment. "Did she love the boy and treat him well?"

"Oh, yes, very. She was extremely rich and lived in Philadelphia. Bradford was raised hearing about his famous father night and day. The grandmother had several portraits and photographs of Fremont from his childhood to his manhood."

Longarm nodded, trying to picture a boy being raised by his grandmother and the ghost of his father.

"To make the impression even more indelible," Julia was saying, "Bradford bears an uncommon resemblance to his late father. The grandmother, Mrs. Alice Gumm, was a widow and she was obsessed by the ghost of her late and famous son. She would stage séances and hold hands with Bradford calling on his father to appear in spirit . . . and most times he would."

Longarm wasn't sure he understood. "Are you saying that Mrs. Buford would claim that her son appeared during these séances?"

"Exactly."

"But . . . but Bradford wouldn't have seen him. I mean, you don't believe that . . ."

"Of course not," Julia said. "But the old woman was a little crazy and also very convincing. I met her before she died and she was spellbinding. It's easy to see how she would have darkened a room, called on the spirit of her son, and then somehow made young and desperately impressionable Bradford believe his father was present."

Julia emptied her glass and motioned for the waiter to bring a second bottle of the best vintage that the railroad had in stock. She pursed her lips together and closed her eyes for a moment before continuing. "I have always thought that the old woman had someone in another room speaking in a low, commanding voice while posing as Fremont P. Gumm."

Longarm poured his own wine. "That would have been a profound experience to a boy yearning to be reunited with his famous father."

"Yes, it would have," Julia agreed. "And Bradford told me that the voice of his father's spirit always told him to become a great man. A famous man. To do impossible things that would further advance the name of the Gumms."

Now Longarm was beginning to understand. "So that is why Bradford went west to find his own fame."

"Yes, it is," Julia sadly concluded. "Oh, I did everything I could to dissuade him from this quest. And Bradford is accomplished, although mostly in terms of his physical prowess. He became an expert marksman, and when he was only eighteen he went on a safari in Africa and killed many huge beasts. Elephants, lions, and rhinoceroses. I am told that he would stand in the face of a charge and wait until the very last moment to fire his rifle and bring down a charging beast of the jungle."

"So he has little or no fear?"

"Not that I have ever seen or heard about. And Bradford is very handsome and intelligent. He could have been a scientist, an artist, a writer, or a famous inventor. Bradford could have gone to work in my father's bank and quickly rose to the position of its president. But he had no interest in business or finance. He was bored with the East and read those awful dime novels by the hundreds. Once, he met Wild Bill Hickok at his tent show and the man autographed a photograph for him. Bradford treasured it and the men talked for hours of the American West."

"I see."

But Julia shook her head. "I doubt that you do, Marshal Long. Were you born and raised in Colorado?"

"No, West Virginia."

"But out in the wilderness, I would bet. Not the city."

"That is true," Longarm admitted. "And after the War Between the States, I came to the West and I've never looked back. Never wanted to return to the place that I was born."

"Well, Bradford never wanted to be born in the East and he always wanted to be a Western lawman or outlaw."

"Outlaw?"

She smiled with amusement. "It was not that Bradford wanted to rob or harm people, but he desperately wanted to be famous. Even more famous than his father."

Longarm nodded, trying to understand all he could about this haunted man, the son of a military hero. He himself was famous, in a manner of speaking. Not as famous as some of the West's most heralded gunmen, but famous enough for his liking. Fame, Longarm had decided very early on in his life, was not nearly what it was cracked up to be. Fame carried with it a heavy responsibility that few men could live up to. Longarm much preferred to be free to move about without causing a stir and absent of all the enemies and jealousies that fame inevitably created.

"Are *you* famous?" Julia was asking. "Is the name of Longarm one to be feared and respected by all?"

"No," Longarm quickly replied.

"It probably means that you are the epitome of the long arm of the law."

"I guess."

"I'm sure of it. Have you killed many men in your line of work?"

"Too many," he said quietly

"How many?"

Longarm was getting upset. "I never kept count and I don't want to remember."

She reached out and touched his arm. "I'm sorry. I've had too much wine and I've forgotten my manners."

"Forget it. And I'm not at all famous," he said, not wanting to be upset or angry. "I suppose I'm well known in certain circles, but not famous."

"You probably have many, many enemies."

"Yes. But fortunately, most of them are either dead or in prison."

"And what about friends?"

"I have only a few."

"You're somewhat of a loner, then?"

The talk was getting a bit too personal, so he just shrugged.

"I'm somewhat of a loner, too," Julia confessed without regret. She drank some more red wine while Longarm stared out the window wondering if he should excuse himself because the woman was drinking too much and talking too much.

Julia broke a long silence. "I am not ashamed to say that I have no real friends. I have family, most of whom I love. But friends . . . well, who needs friends? They turn on you. They disappoint you and they are always gossiping behind your back and usually filled with envy."

Longarm took a deep drink. The second bottle was emptying fast and he realized that he badly needed to take a piss. "I'd better be leaving," he said, starting to rise.

But she grabbed his arm and turned her face to his so that it was close. "Do you wonder *why* I so love Bradford?"

The question had been on his mind, but Longarm said, "It's none of my business."

Julia's eyes twinkled with merriment. "The woman that caused you to be two hours late and sucked like a little vampire on your neck. Do you love her deeply?"

"I . . . I don't," he admitted, seeing no reason to lie.

She looked down at the table and he was sure that his

answer was not to her liking. "How disappointing . . . and also how very . . . interesting."

"Whatever, ma'am. I have to go now."

"Before you leave, please know that I love Bradford very much. You must remember that at all times."

"I will," he promised.

"There will be times when I act like I don't love him . . . but I do."

"Sure. Anything you say."

She winked. "Just so you understand, Marshal. And you don't forget."

"I won't, Miss Konrad. That much I'll promise."

She nodded with exaggeration. "Then this conversation has been very worthwhile . . . very productive."

His bladder was about to burst. "Please excuse me."

"Of course," she said, lifting the bottle up to candle-light. "I can finish the rest of this all by myself."

Despite the urgency of his situation, Longarm paused a moment to say, "See you in the morning, Miss Konrad. Try to get a good night's sleep because we'll be getting off this train tomorrow in Flagstaff and from there until we reach Pine Valley could be a hard journey."

"I'm up to it," she told him, words slightly slurred. "I know that you don't believe that, but I'll show you what I'm made of."

"Glad to hear that," he told her as he left the table wondering what in the hell had been going on in Julia's mind and what kind of a grandmother would trick her grandson in such a despicable and twisted manner.

Longarm didn't know if Bradford G. Gumm was dead or alive, but now he knew that the man was bound to be a bit odd . . . or at least eccentric.

"Marshal Long?"

It was the porter, a short, balding man with a quick but insincere smile. "Yes?"

"The lady left this note to be given to you in private after you dined with her."

The note was enclosed in an envelope of the finest stationery and sealed with a wax stamp. "Thank you."

The porter nodded and left. After taking a most satisfactory leak, Longarm adjourned to his private first-class compartment and locked the door. He sat down and turned on his lamp so that he could read the note. It was short and shocking.

If my Bradford is dead, I want you, *Marshal Custis Long, also known as the famous and fearless Longarm.*

He stared at the note and reread it twice again. "Strange, strange woman," he said aloud. "And if Bradford is dead, I could be in deep, deep trouble."

Chapter 5

Early the next morning, Longarm was awakened by the screech of iron wheels locking on iron rails as the train braked. He was almost thrown off his small bed and couldn't imagine what was going on. Perhaps the train had come across another damaged trestle and had been forced to make an emergency stop to avoid crashing into some remote ravine. Or maybe the train had hit another cow, or perhaps a tree had fallen across the rails. And finally, there was always the chance that the locomotive's boiler had exploded . . . or that the train was being held up by a gang of thieves.

Longarm quickly pulled on his boots and shirt, then strapped on his gun and finally shrugged into his vest and coat. The train was now fully stopped, and he peered out through his compartment window to see five masked horsemen in the act of forcing the conductor and a porter off the train.

"Damn," he swore, wondering how many other train robbers might be involved that he could not yet see.

Longarm had a shotgun and a Winchester in the big satchel that he had carried on board, and now he grabbed the shotgun thinking that it would be the more effective weapon against so many. The thing about his shotgun was that it almost always scared the piss out of anyone who had the misfortune of looking down its big double barrels. On the other hand, as he peered through the curtains, Longarm could see that at least two of the thieves also had weapons similar to his own.

Longarm checked the shotgun and then decided to also take the Winchester. He could always drop it in the aisle if it wasn't needed in a fight. And it never hurt to have too many weapons. So between the rifle, the shotgun, his pistol, and his hideout derringer, Longarm knew that he was packing one hell of a lot of firepower.

As Longarm exited his train compartment, he ran smack into one of the porters, who was already white-faced with fear and so nervous that he could hardly speak.

"Take it easy," Longarm said to the poor man. "Tell me how many outlaws we have to stop."

"Six . . . I think. Two outside and four others that have boarded the train and are starting to force everyone off."

Longarm took a deep breath. He wasn't afraid of confronting the train robbers, but on the other hand, if some of the passengers were already off the train and among the thieves, he might be risking their lives in a full-blown shootout. One thing for sure, he wouldn't be able to use the shotgun because it would surely injure or kill passengers along with the thieves. Shotguns were not very choosy about their victims, cutting down the good and the bad with equal deadly efficiency.

"What are we going to do, Marshal!"

"I'm thinking. Take a deep breath and try to be calm," Longarm advised, seeing that the porter was in his fifties and gray in the face. "There is no point in you having heart trouble on top of everything else."

Longarm expelled a deep breath and gathered his thoughts. "Go through all the first-class coaches and tell the passengers to lock their compartments and stay inside. The thieves will want to rob them first knowing that they have the most money and jewels."

"Yes, sir!" The porter swung his head around when he heard an angry shout and then the blast of a six-gun. "Oh, Gawd, they're going to murder all the passengers up front!"

"Tell them to lock their doors!" Longarm ordered. "And hold onto this shotgun for me because I may need it in a hurry."

The man stared at the formidable weapon and his eyes grew round with fear. "You expect *me* to shoot them?"

"As a matter of fact, if it comes to it, I damn sure do."

The man shoved the weapon back at Longarm shaking his head and saying, "I'm just a porter. I don't want to get shot to death."

Longarm shoved the porter backward with disgust. "Then just tell everyone in first class to lock their doors and sit tight."

"What about all the ones back in second and third class that ain't got any compartments?"

"If any of them are armed and have the guts to fight, tell them to come on forward and give me some support. The rest should just stay in their seats. Try to keep the women and children calm."

"Yes, sir! I'll do that, Marshal."

Longarm didn't see how the terrified porter could help anyone be calm when he himself was so scared he looked like he might faint or fall over dead with fright.

"I'll take that shotgun," Julia Konrad said, stepping into the car and reaching for the weapon.

"Not a chance," Longarm told her. "Go back to your compartment and lock your door. Now you can see why I wanted you to leave your jewels in Denver."

"Which I did . . . at least most of them. But I'm not going to just hide right now like some scared rabbit while you try to shoot it out with a band of desperate train robbers."

"Julia, please," he said, furious because this was wasting precious time. "Just . . . just let me deal with this the best way that I can. People are probably going to die in the next few minutes and the very last thing I need is for you to be one of them."

Longarm left her standing there without a weapon and with her mouth open as she began to protest. Whatever she was going to say, he did not have the time or the patience to hear of it.

The first train robber was standing over an older couple who were lying down in the aisle. The man had been pistol-whipped and the woman was screaming and nearly hysterical. Longarm didn't waste any time or thought in asking the robber to drop his gun, but instead shot him in the head with his pistol, dropping him in the aisle beside the older couple. To Longarm's surprise and dismay, the sight of brains and blood completely unhinged the old couple.

"Sorry about the mess," Longarm said, climbing over the bunch of them and then moving down the aisle toward the next car with the Winchester in his left hand, his pistol in his right hand and shotgun on his shoulder.

In the next car he saw three of the train robbers at work. Again, he wasted no time with a warning, but instead opened fire on them where they stood. His first bullet

46

caught one of the thieves in the neck sending him to the Promised Land, and his second bullet caught a big, bearded thief square in the chest. This masked man peered stupidly down at his coat and the spurting blood of his heart. Then he raised his head and stared at Longarm and shouted a terrible curse, so Longarm shot him in the mask and he crashed over backward into the third train robber.

This man had a little more warning than his two companions, and he ducked and fired in one smooth motion. Longarm felt a bullet crease his arm, and then a second bullet whistled past his ear to shatter a lamp. Longarm drilled the man through the forehead. It was a brain shot and it stood the thief up and made him look to heaven for an instant before he tumbled forward dead and landed on the big, bearded thief, who was still twitching in death.

There was blood all over the place and people were screaming like crazy. Longarm shouted for them to settle down and try to be calm, but no one could hear his voice, so he marched on through the carnage. When he came to the platform between the cars, he peered out and saw a man on horseback who was being handed canvas sacks of money and jewelry by a man on foot.

"Hey!" Longarm yelled.

The man on the horse twisted around in his saddle and saw Longarm, who had holstered his gun and was now cocking both hammers of the shotgun. The other man, who had been handing up the bounty, froze in disbelief and then went for his six-gun.

Longarm unleashed a blast from one of the barrels of the shotgun. He purposely aimed high so that he could avoid hitting the horse. But some of the shot must have at least nicked the animal, and when its rider was slammed out of his saddle in a spray of flesh and blood, the horse began to buck and jump as if it had a burr under its saddle blanket.

Fortunately, the crazed horse slammed into the one on foot and knocked him down hard on the roadbed. Longarm raised the shotgun and smiled as he squeezed the second trigger. "So long, you thieving sonofabitch!"

"No! No, please!"

The blast from the shotgun kicked the thief like the hooves of a Missouri mule, and the man skidded across the cinder track bed with very little left of his upper body still recognizable.

Longarm jumped down from the train and dropped his empty shotgun as he hurried over to the dead men thinking that he had killed every last damn one of them, and had been remarkably fortunate that he'd not also killed at least one innocent passenger or two.

"You sonofabitch!" one more masked thief screamed emerging from the locomotive with his gun raised.

Longarm realized he'd missed this one, and his hand stabbed downward for his gun as he threw himself down on the track bed. He felt cinders being kicked into his eyes, and was momentarily blinded as the last train robber tried to finish him off.

But suddenly a smaller-caliber pistol was barking and when Longarm could clear his vision, he saw that the last gunman was shot and dying.

"Who . . . ?"

Julia Konrad had a small pistol in her fist and her hand and arm were steady, even if her face was drained and pale.

"You?" Longarm asked with disbelief.

"I told you I could shoot. Good thing, too, or you'd be dead right now."

Longarm wiped blood and cinders from his face and

climbed a bit unsteadily to his feet. "I hope that's the last of them," he managed to say as he trudged over to the train and sat down heavily on the platform step. "I feel like a cat that has used up all its nine lives for today."

"You've been hit."

"It's only a crease," he assured her. "Nothing that a little bandage won't cure."

"I'll be the judge of that," Julia said, helping him back to his feet. "And do you have any idea of the mess that you've caused?"

"Some. Lot's of dead men and lots of blood."

"It's a sight that I thought I'd never have to see," Julia announced. "I almost wish you'd just let them rob all of us and then . . ."

"I couldn't do that," he told her. "It's my job to try to stop things like this from happening. And maybe they'd have shot some people just out of spite. They were bad ones."

"But couldn't you have gotten the drop on them and made arrests?"

Longarm shook his head. "What do you honestly think would have happened if I'd have given them the least bit of warning?"

"They'd have shot you dead," Julia heard herself say.

Longarm pulled his pocket watch out of his vest, which was covered with blood. He would have to toss the vest and coat away. "It's only a little after seven o'clock in the morning."

"So what!"

"So it's earlier than usual for a drink," Longarm explained, "but just for this morning, I'm going to make an exception."

They were entering the coach where Longarm had shot

49

three train robbers down in the aisle. It was chaos and women and children were wailing, while most of the men sat looking stunned, although a few were trying to comfort their families.

"Sorry about all this," Longarm said loudly. "Won't happen again, you can be sure of it."

"How the hell *could* it happen again?" a man asked, shaking his head. "You killed every last damn one of them."

"No," Longarm said, correcting the man, "I killed six and this lady beside me got the last one. I give credit where credit is due."

The man was heavyset and prosperous-looking with expensive gold jewelry and manicured fingernails. Maybe a banker or a lawyer to Longarm's way of thinking. The passenger shook his head as if chasing away a daze and said to Julia, "Miss, did you really kill one of them?"

"I did and I'm not sorry."

"Well, I'm not either," the heavyset man agreed, nodding his head up and down and shaking his jowls. "In fact, I'm awful damned glad of it, miss. And I think when this train arrives at the next stop, you and the marshal here are going to become heroes. I tell you the telegraph lines are going to be humming for hours after this!"

Longarm and Julia said nothing.

The heavyset man pulled out a silver pen and pad of paper. "What are your full names?"

Longarm didn't really want to give out his name. He suspected that the heavyset man was right about the tide of publicity this slaughter would generate all the way to the East and West Coasts. And Billy Vail would hear about it and think that it was insane.

"I'd rather not give my name," Longarm said.

"Oh, but you must! You're an officer of the law, are you not?"

"I am, but. . . ."

"Then you simply must!"

Longarm knew this was true so he told the man his name.

He turned to Julia. "And yours, miss?"

Julia Konrad didn't hesitate giving the gentleman her full name, and then she said, "I'm engaged to be married to Bradford G. Gumm and that's why I'm on this train . . . to find and be married to him. So if this is to be newsworthy, I want to make sure that you note that I am looking for my fiancé. I'll repeat and even spell his name out for you."

"Is he by any chance related to the great Major Forrest P. Gumm?"

Julia managed a smile. "Bradford is his only son."

"Well, this is *really* going to be a story!" The heavyset man stuck out his chubby fist. "My name is Mortimer P. Orman. I'm the publisher of the . . ."

Longarm didn't wait to hear what newspaper the man was the publisher of because he was already stomping out of the coach and heading through the cars toward his own compartment.

The thing of it was that he didn't like the smell or the sight of fresh blood on his clothing. Also, he really did need to take a few good strong drinks and the early hour be damned.

Chapter 6

True to his word, newspaper publisher Mortimer P. Orman had sent out a long and detailed telegram about the botched New Mexico train robbery and shootout. And so by the time the train arrived at their final departing point of Flagstaff, Arizona, there was a huge mob of people waiting just to catch a glimpse of the famous lawman and the soon-to-be bride of Bradford G. Gumm. It was a sensational event and the story had created a massive amount of interest from coast to coast.

"Look at that!" Longarm groused as he peered out the train's window when it neared the station. "There must be five hundred people standing there and you can bet they're not all waiting to greet friends and family."

Julia nodded, looking pleased. "I was hoping for five thousand, but I guess that was too much to expect in a town this small. But I would say there are over a thousand."

"That's just dandy," Longarm said with disgust. "It'll make my job in Pine Valley all the tougher."

"Maybe not," Julia said as the train slowed at the station. "After all, whoever is fighting this so-called range war is probably going to hear about your reputation and won't want to cross you under any circumstances. Marshal Long, like it or not, you are as famous as Billy the Kid and probably considered every bit as deadly."

"Billy was a back-shooter and cold-blooded killer who was finally gunned down by the sheriff of Lincoln County, New Mexico, Pat Garrett . . . a man I know and respect." Longarm studied the crowd with growing displeasure. "Julia, I'm going to slip out on the far side of this train to avoid this circus. I'll meet you at the Hotel Monte Vista in about an hour."

"But. . . ."

"I'm going to find out about transportation to Pine Valley. Maybe there's a stagecoach running down to there, but most likely not. We might have to rent or even buy some horses."

"I'd much prefer to travel in a comfortable carriage."

"I'm sure you would," Longarm told her. "But if we have to walk, we're still going to get there and we need to leave just as soon as possible."

"I agree. But I want a carriage or buggy and I'm willing to pay for it myself."

"I'll keep that in mind," Longarm said, grabbing his bags and moving up the aisle as the train ground to a shuddering halt.

"Marshal, I just can't understand why you won't meet those people!" Julia called after him. "They'll be far more interested in your story than mine."

"No, they won't," Longarm yelled over his shoulder a moment before he jumped down on the off side of the train where no one was waiting.

He ducked down and peered under the train and saw the hundreds of feet and legs of the anxiously waiting crowd.

Longarm smiled because he was glad that he had missed all those people. Mostly they would want to see the dead train robbers when they were carted off to the local undertaker. People loved to look at dead outlaws, and the bloodier they were the better. Longarm didn't understand that . . . between the war and his profession, he had already seen more than enough dead people to last ten lifetimes.

Longarm made his way up San Francisco Street until he came to a livery that looked promising because it advertised "horses, mules, and all manners of reliable conveyance for hire." The sign also had the proprietor's name printed in bold letters. P.J. Thompson.

"Are you Mr. Thompson?" Longarm asked a short, dirty little man who was about to rope a strawberry roan in a pine-pole corral.

"Wish I were!" the man shouted back as the roan swept past him. "But I'm just the poor hired help. P.J. is inside the office inside the barn."

"Much obliged," Longarm said.

"Watch your wallet, mister!"

At just that moment the little wrangler whirled his rope twice and sent it spinning out to drop over the roan's head. Longarm paused as the roan, suddenly captured, turned as gentle as a plow horse.

"Nice toss!"

"Thank you. Want to polish him off for me?"

"Nope," Longarm said, heading for the barn to meet the proprietor.

P.J. Thompson was a man in his mid-seventies with a good head of silver hair and mustache to match. He was seated in a chair with his feet up on a keg of horseshoes and he was reading a fresh newspaper. He wore a faded blue-denim shirt and red suspenders, and spectacles rested deep down on his nose.

"Mr. Thompson?"

He looked up, in no hurry. "That's me, sonny. And who might you be?"

"Deputy Marshal Custis Long from Denver." Longarm showed the man his badge.

P.J. took it and studied it carefully before he looked up and said, "You're the big hero, I suppose. The one who just gunned down ten train robbers."

"I only killed six."

"That's a mighty big 'only,'" P.J. said, drawing a half-smoked cigar out of his shirt pocket and lighting it with a match against his thumbnail. "You must be one helluva cool customer."

In contrast to most people, Longarm never liked to talk about himself. "Is there a stagecoach running out of this town?"

"Yep. Goes to Prescott every other day."

"I need to get down to Pine Valley."

"With that woman I read about? The one that is lookin' for Major Fremont Gumm's lost son?"

"I guess you've read the article, huh?"

"Sure have. That's what I'm reading right now. And you'd be wanting to rent something to drive down to Pine Valley and find that younger Gumm fella, huh?"

"I would."

"Doesn't seem to have the sense of a goose," P.J. said. "But he must have something good about him or that woman wouldn't have come so far."

"I expect he does."

P.J. neatly folded his newspaper and then stood. He

was about a foot shorter than Longarm, but he still had broad shoulders and a thick neck telling Longarm that he'd done more than his share of hard physical work in his long lifetime.

"Are you aware, Marshal Long, that there is a bloody range war going on down in Pine Valley?"

"I am."

"And are you also aware that some of those jaspers down there will shoot a stranger on sight just assuming he is hired by the opposition?"

"I didn't think of that."

"Well, you should," P.J. said bluntly. "And that woman that killed the train robber and can't find her man should know it, too."

"We're still going down there," Longarm said, "and I need some way to reach Pine Valley. Preferably by a carriage, but even a buckboard will do."

The old livery owner shook his head. "That's the *worst* thing you could go by, if you ask me."

"Why is that?"

"Because you'd *both* be easy targets. Better to ride horses and travel light and fast. That way, if you get in a jam, you can still make a run for it. Might get lucky and get away clean."

"I'm not looking for the fastest way *out* of Pine Valley," Longarm told the old man. "I'm looking for the fastest way *into* Pine Valley."

"Exactly what I'm sayin'! What you need to do is to buy a couple of real fast horses from me. Nothin' but the best or you'll get caught for certain. I'll guarantee you that those boys on either side of the feud won't appreciate the law coming down to their valley. And as for that pistol-packin' Miss Konrad . . . they won't be impressed. Why, I've heard that there are women down in Pine Valley walkin' around with guns on their hips and notches on their guns!"

Longarm could easily see where this conversation was headed. P.J. was setting him up to think that he needed nothing but the best and fastest animals available, and that meant the most expensive.

"I don't want to buy horses," Longarm said, hoping to head off the sales pitch. "I want to rent two reliable horses to pull a carriage."

P.J. just shook his head as if Longarm were the stupidest man alive. "Are you hard of hearin', Marshal? You must be because you don't seem to be listenin' to what I'm trying to tell you."

"I've heard you, Mr. Thompson," Longarm said, getting peevish, "and I'm thinking that I'll go find another livery. A town this big has to have several and the next one maybe won't try to tell me how to go about my business."

Longarm turned and started to leave, but the old livery-man was after him in a flash. "All right! All damn right!" he complained. "We'll do it your way, but I just had to clear my conscience by explaining the facts. I was just trying to save your hide, Marshal. And that of the Eastern lady. But since you won't listen, I won't say another word except to say that I just happen to have two of the finest horses you could hope to buy in any town at any price."

"And they'll pull a carriage or buggy?"

"I . . . I don't know. They're *racehorses,* Marshal. But I suppose Skeeter out there could manage to harness them to a buggy and then, if you were to get them headed in exactly the proper direction, you'd have yourself a real fine pair and you'd make it down to Pine Valley in record time."

Longarm wasn't too excited about racehorses. "What if I *rented* them?"

"Nope." P.J. folded his arms over his barrel chest. "It's likely that I'll never see you, the lady, or those horses again. If you deal with me, Marshal, it's a buy-'em-for-*cash* deal."

Longarm frowned and considered the situation. He could go around to other liveries, but something told him he'd have a problem renting horses given his sudden fame and published destination.

"Let me take a look at the horses."

P.J. grinned to show that he still had a full set of teeth. "Sure enough, but just remember that when you want the best, you got to pay the most."

"Yeah, right," Longarm said, wondering if Julia would chip in a wad of cash for two top-quality racing horses.

Skeeter had the roan tied to a post in the center of the corral and the horse was snubbed down close. When his boss told him that he wanted the racehorses saddled, Skeeter obviously had no idea what the man was talking about.

"You know," P.J. groused as if the man were a moron, "those two chestnuts that I bought just last week."

"Those two?"

"Sure!" P.J. said, looking mad enough to bite through nails. "Saddle and bridle them and then ride 'em around for the marshal here. Show him how well they handle."

Skeeter's eyes widened a little, and he had to clamp his lips shut before he marched off to follow orders.

"Skeeter," P.J. said, "is a good hand with horses. Best I ever saw, but he's kinda slow to figure out things. I reckon he was bounced out of the saddle and onto his head once too often."

"Either that or he thinks you're wrong to try to pass those horses off on me and a lady."

"Naw! It ain't nothin' like that, Marshal! You wait until you see this pair. They're both tall and handsome . . . like yourself."

"Flattery won't get you a thing, P.J.," Longarm told the man. "And I doubt that I'll want these horses."

"You will when you see 'em."

Longarm wanted to go around the barn and watch Skeeter catch and saddle the horses, but P.J. kept jawin' so steadily that he couldn't get away from the liveryman. Twenty minutes later, here came Skeeter leading the saddled chestnuts, and Longarm had to blink with admiration because they were a fine pair of animals. Tall and handsome, just as promised.

But they were also spirited and jumping around.

"Give me one of 'em and then get up in the saddle and ride the other," P.J. ordered.

Skeeter gave the old man a go-to-hell look as he screwed his hat down tight and then jammed his boot into the stirrup and swung on board. The chestnut stood still and when Skeeter gave it a nudge with his boot heels, the animal walked out as nice as anything.

"See!" P.J. said, obviously relieved. "Skeeter, trot him around and then put him into a gallop around my barn."

Skeeter did as he was ordered, and Longarm saw the big chestnut go trotting around the huge barn. Only thing was, when the chestnut reappeared, there was no Skeeter still on board.

"What happened to him!" Longarm said, rushing over to grab the chestnut's dragging reins. The animal was rolling its eyes and crow-hopping around the place scattering ducks, dogs, and chickens.

"The old fool must have fell off," P.J. complained. "He

ain't much good at anything anymore. Don't know why I keep him around."

Longarm had seen enough. "Here," he said, handing the reins to P.J. and stomping away. "I'll go someplace else for horses and a buggy."

"Wait!"

Longarm knew he shouldn't have stopped, but the desperation in P.J.'s voice drew him up short. He turned and said, "Mister, are you finally through trying to horse-trade me out of a pile of money and into a pile of misery?"

"I got a couple of nice older horses. Can't run more'n half a mile, but they'll pull a buggy all day and everyday. And I'll sell them cheap if you buy the buggy and harness from me and not someone else."

"How much?"

"A hundred dollars for all of it. Hell of a deal."

"Too much," Longarm said, starting to turn.

"All right, dammit! Seventy-five for the two horses, the buggy, and the harness. I'll even throw in two hundred pounds of oats and tell you that you've skinned me good."

"Let's see what you have," Longarm said. "It might work."

"These geldings will take you to Pine Valley for sure. Only thing is that a kid on a cow could outrun 'em should it become necessary for you to try to run for your life."

"I'm not interested in running," Longarm said. "I stand my ground."

P.J. smiled unexpectedly. "So I read. And so does that lady from back East."

"Time is wasting, P.J. Let's get down to business."

"You must be in a big hurry to die, Marshal."

Longarm didn't reply as he followed P.J. around the

61

barn to find Skeeter on his back moaning in pain. "Are you hurt badly?" Longarm asked the little wrangler.

"No more than usual. Did you catch up that red sonofabitchin' horse?"

"We did."

"Good, 'cause I'm going to go find my gun and shoot him full of holes."

"Oh, shut up, Skeeter," P.J. said, coming up behind leading his "racehorses." "Just catch up old Jessie and old Shorty and hitch 'em up to that buggy I bought last month . . . if you can still move and still want to work for me."

Skeeter muttered something under his breath as Longarm helped the poor man to his feet.

"He's a sonofabitch to work for," Skeeter said quietly enough so that his boss couldn't hear. "But we been friends for nearly forty years and nobody else is offerin' me work these days."

"Are Jessie and Shorty reliable?"

"Steady and as slow as pregnant buffalo," he replied. "You can't go wrong with 'em, but you'll be tryin' to make 'em go faster all the time."

"And what about the buggy he wants me to buy?"

"It's sound as a dollar and in fine condition."

Longarm nodded with understanding. "How is the road down to Pine Valley?"

"Awful."

"But passable?"

"You'll make it, Marshal. But I just don't know why you'd want to. Them folks in Pine Valley are all tetchy as teased snakes and so poor that most of 'em are about as fat as a needle. I hear that they're all crazier than shit-house rats, but they can shoot the eyes off a gnat on the wing."

"Sounds like we're not going to be real welcome in Pine Valley."

"About as welcome as a skunk at a picnic."

Longarm sighed. "Well, Skeeter, we're going there anyway and we're going to get things settled."

"Good luck and good-bye," the man said, shaking his head sadly. "Marshal, if you have any kinfolks you want notified, then write down their names and addresses and I'll see they get your message."

"Thanks," Longarm told the hobbling wrangler, "but I'm pretty much in this life alone and by choice."

"Amen," Skeeter said, "I understand you, brother."

Chapter 7

Longarm wasn't too excited about traveling in a slow-moving buggy, and yet he understood that Miss Julia might not do well riding a horse through rough country and facing the risk of bad weather. So he agreed to buy the old horses, buggy, and harness, then went to find Miss Konrad at the hotel.

If he had hoped and expected to find her alone in her room, he was in for a surprise because the woman was in the lobby surrounded by admiring men, many of them local politicians and hopeful bachelors. Longarm took one glance into the lobby at the crowd and started to turn and leave, but Julia spotted him and called, "Oh, Marshal Custis Long. Please come in and join us."

"I'd rather not," Longarm said in his typically blunt fashion. "But I do need to speak to you in private . . . if it's not too damned inconvenient."

Julia's smile melted and her eyes sparked with anger. Then she turned to her admirers and said, "Obviously, United States Marshal Long is a man of few words and even fewer good manners. But he is unquestionably one of the bravest individuals I've ever known."

Many of the reporters converged on Custis, all of them wanting to hear his version of what happened on the train.

"Tell us exactly how you gunned each man down," one of the reporters pleaded. "And don't worry about shocking anyone. My readers want the bloody truth and nothing less will do."

Longarm shook his head with resignation. He was sure that, if he didn't at least give these people some account, then they would hound him unmercifully. "I'm assuming that Miss Konrad told you that I shot six men and the seventh would have probably gotten me if she hadn't shot him first. As for the details, well, everything just happened so fast that it's going to take me a while to sort things out."

"Marshal, are you aware that this gang had robbed other trains and killed passengers?" a man asked. "And that there is a large reward on their heads?"

"No," Longarm replied, "I had not been aware of that."

"The reward is a hundred dollars a man . . . dead or alive. That means that you've earned six hundred dollars, Marshal Long."

"Because I'm a U.S. lawman, you must know that I can't accept the money," Longarm explained. "I would ask that it be divided equally among the survivors of the passengers that died at the hands of these thieves. But perhaps Miss Konrad *will* accept her reward."

"No," Julia said, chin lifting. "I too would prefer to see the money go to the families of those that were killed by those ruthless thieves."

There was a scattering of applause and then someone called out, "When are you and the marshal going down to Pine Valley?"

Julia exchanged glances with Longarm, who said, "I was sent by my superiors from Denver to put an end to the range war and to find Marshal Gumm, who I understand was deputized."

"Is the man qualified to be a United States marshal?" someone in the crowd asked.

"I am told that he is."

"Of course he is!" Julia added, clearly angered at the question. "Bradford is a crack shot and well able to handle himself in any kind of trouble."

"But he hasn't even been heard from in . . . what?"

"A few months," Julia had to admit. "But that doesn't mean that he isn't down there trying to do his job. Why, he might even have settled that bloody conflict and be on his way back by now."

A tall man wearing a fine Stetson stepped forward. "No offense, Miss Konrad, but I do happen to know a thing or two about Pine Valley and that feud that is going on right now between the sheep men and the cattlemen. And I can tell you with dead certainty that neither side is about to let an outsider . . . even one with a star pinned on his chest . . . interfere. And if your intended hasn't been heard from in months, you can bet he's pushing up sod in some unmarked grave."

Julia paled a little and seemed to be at a rare loss for words. Longarm felt sorry for her, so he said, "It's true that Marshal Gumm might have been killed or injured. But it's also true that he might have gone undercover."

"Undercover?" the tall man asked.

"That's right," Longarm said. "It wouldn't be the first time that a federal marshal had to assume some identity other than his own in order to get the information he needed to make future arrests."

"Have you ever gone undercover?" the man demanded.

"As a matter of fact," Longarm said, "I have . . . but

only when to have done otherwise would have caused me or someone else to be murdered."

The lobby fell silent as everyone digested this news. Suddenly, one of the reporters shouted, "Could you tell us about when this happened? Give us some stories to write, Marshal Long. This is hot news . . . you going undercover. I didn't know that you were allowed to do that."

Longarm singled out the reporter, who was young and looked both excited and inexperienced. "I can't tell you when or where I've done that because there are still people whose lives might be threatened by that information. I can only say that we are sworn to uphold the law and sometimes that calls for unusual methods."

"When are you leaving for Pine Valley?"

"How about today?" Longarm asked, eyes locked on Julia.

"How about tomorrow morning," she said. "I am tired and unwilling to travel any further today."

Had they been alone, Longarm would have probably put his foot down hard and insisted they leave immediately. But the two horses, buggy, and harness were going to cost a lot more than he'd expected and he needed the woman's funds to help defer the cost, so he said, "All right."

Julia was caught off guard because she'd been expecting an argument. "Good," she managed to say.

"I'll still need to talk to you in private," Longarm insisted.

Julia nodded and turned to the group. "Gentlemen, it has been a very long and dangerous day. I need to excuse myself and attend to my rest and refreshment."

There was a groan of disappointment, and then Julia came over joined Longarm with a smile. "Will you please escort me up to my room, Marshal?"

"Sure," he said curtly.

On their way up the stairs a dozen questions were shouted at them, but Julia did not acknowledge a single one and neither did Custis.

"You aren't very good at interviews, are you?" she said in the upstairs hallway.

"Nope."

"You ought to improve your manners and comportment with the public. If you did, you might find that good things would happen for you."

"I'm too stubborn to change my ways, Miss Konrad."

"I can see that." Julia came to her door. "Did you find us a suitable means of transportation?"

"I did. I had to buy a buggy and a couple of horses."

"I'll reimburse you."

"Better yet," he said, "why don't you pay for them in the morning."

"That would be fine." She smiled. "I knew that you wouldn't try to force me to ride a horse, which would be very unladylike."

"We might have to yet," he told her. "And by the way, I sure wish that everyone in this part of Arizona didn't know our exact plan and timetable. The publicity we faced today will make things far more difficult."

"So you've told me. I just happen to disagree."

"Why?" Longarm asked.

"Because, if anyone has any bad intentions in mind, then this publicity will give them second thoughts."

"Well," Longarm said, "that's an interesting theory. Too bad that it's all wet."

Julia glared up at him. "It's such a shame that such a handsome and brave man as yourself is so difficult. If you had a better personality, Marshal, you could just about write you own ticket in life. You could be successful."

"I am already successful," Longarm snapped, "only not by your standards, which are money and social status."

Julia started to say something, then changed her mind and opened her door. "I think I've about heard enough from you today, Marshal Long. Good night."

"Good night," he said, not bothering to remove his hat.

After she shut her door, Longarm stood for a minute in silence trying to beat down his anger and exasperation. He honestly didn't know how he was going to put up with this obstinate and overbearing bitch for the next week or two, and he just hated the fact that she was unwittingly doing her best to get them both killed.

Chapter 8

"Marshal Custis Long?"

Longarm thought that Julia was calling him from her doorway wanting to get in the last word. Instead, it was a young woman that he had never seen before. She had red hair and was wearing a riding habit, yellow scarf, and riding boots. She was shapely, and he immediately knew by her tanned good looks that she was not a hotel prostitute hoping to lure him into her room.

"You talking to me?" he asked.

"Yes," she replied, softly shutting her door and tiptoeing up the hallway to extend her hand. "I've been hoping to speak to you in private, but you always seem to be surrounded either by Miss Konrad or the newspaper people."

"Not always," he said, keeping his voice down because she was whispering. "What's this about?"

"It's very important we talk," she said. "Will you come to my room for a moment?"

On more than one occasion in his dangerous career, Longarm had been lured into a hotel room by a strange and attractive female only to be pounced upon by enemies. So now, he was cautious about the offer.

"What is this about, miss?"

"It's about Bradford Gumm, of course. I might be able to help you find him."

"I already know where to find him. He's in Pine Valley."

"Are you sure?" She smiled and cocked her head a little to one side. "Or is that just the last place that Bradford was known to be?"

"Maybe we should talk," Longarm said in a low voice.

"I promise that you won't be wasting your time. I even have some very good whiskey and I have always hated to drink alone."

Longarm had to grin as he nodded and followed her into her room at the far end of the hallway. "Me, too."

His hand was inside his coat and his thumb was on the hammer of his hideout derringer when he entered the room. Longarm did a quick inspection, and then relaxed because there was no one else waiting.

"You look tired, Marshal. Why don't you take off your coat and hat and sit in that big easy chair while I pour us some of that whiskey?"

"Sounds like a good idea."

While she turned and reached for a bottle, Longarm surveyed the woman closer. She was probably in her late twenties and she already had faint crows-feet lines at the corners of her eyes telling him she'd spent most of her time outdoors. She moved with an easy, economical grace, and he was sure that she was ranch-raised. That suspicion was confirmed when his eyes happened to fall on a beautiful silver inlaid bit and bridle that was hanging on a hat tree under a rain slicker and battered gray Stetson hat.

"Here you go," she said with a smile as she turned to face him. "To successful and safe manhunting."

They clicked glasses and Longarm took a drink. The

woman hadn't lied. This was excellent whiskey even if the toast itself was odd.

"And to us," she added.

"Sure. Why not? To us."

Longarm drank a second time, and realized that his whiskey glass was empty. "May I ask your name?"

"Miss Cynthia Holden."

"And you're not a town girl. In fact, you're a ranch girl."

"That's right," she replied.

"*And*," he stressed, "I'll just bet you're from Pine Valley and you came all the way up here to Flagstaff because of Mr. Gumm."

"My," she said, without sounding condescending, "aren't you the clever lawman? So far, you're right on all counts."

She refilled their glasses and pulled a chair up close. "But you only know the half of it, Marshal Long."

"Custis," he corrected. "I don't drink with people that won't call me by my first name unless they're outlaws and enemies. And you don't strike me as being an outlaw and I sure hope you're not my enemy."

"Quite the opposite," she said, tossing her red hair. "I'm up here in Flagstaff for one reason and one reason only."

"And that is?"

She smiled sweetly. "I'm here to save your ass. Pardon my bluntness, but that's the long and short of it."

Longarm shook his head and studied the woman. "Why don't you start from the beginning and tell me what this is all about."

"It's all about Bradford. Who else? He and I met in Pine Valley on the very first day he arrived."

"Well, at least now I know he wasn't shot the first day he got there."

73

"No, he wasn't. Actually, Marshal, I instantly fell in love with him and he fell in love with me . . . unfortunately, it only lasted for a short while."

Longarm frowned. "Are you serious?"

"As a sinner in church."

"But didn't Gumm tell you that he was engaged to be married to Miss Konrad?"

"He did." Cynthia looked away for a moment as if remembering every word. "Bradford said that he had never really loved Miss Konrad. He swore to me that he needed to get away from Washington and all that high society so that he could have time to clear his head and think of a way to gracefully get out of that marriage."

"How do I know that this is true? Because, if it is, it changes almost everything."

"What I've told you is the truth. Bradford and I were lovers. But then I realized that he would never be happy living on my family's ranch . . . or even one that we could buy somewhere far away. You see, Marshal, Bradford fancies himself as a man's man and wants to be famous on the frontier, but he's really a city fella. I tried not to see that, but it couldn't be ignored, and so I broke off the relationship."

"Whoa!" Longarm said, raising his hand. "You're going too fast."

"Do you want a few intimate details? If so, I can tell you that Bradford has a big mole right beside—"

"Never mind."

"Okay, then I can show you a couple of love letters he wrote to me after I told him that it wasn't going to work out between us."

"I've never seen his handwriting and so they wouldn't mean anything to me," Longarm told her.

"Then how about this?" Cynthia went over to a drawer

and removed a daguerreotype of the two of them standing close together. Bradford's arm rested over Cynthia's shoulder and even though the image was of poor quality, it was clear to Longarm that the man was looking adoringly at Cynthia.

"All right. Let's say that I do believe that he came out here and fell in love with you at first sight. What about the range war?"

"It's still going on. There's still a few on both sides that are standing. Not many, but a few."

"But you're not part of it?"

"I should say not," she told him. "We're much too smart for that. You see, my family ranches about forty miles east of Pine Valley. Our water rights don't conflict with anyone else's and our cattle are fenced in with miles of barbed wire. We've always treated our neighbors with respect and kept them at a distance. Bradford found this out when he was wounded and—"

"Wounded?"

"That's right. He came into Pine Valley and told everyone he was a federal officer of the law. He called both sides of the feud to come to a meeting and promised that he'd help them iron out their differences. He said that, if they didn't come, he'd start arresting people and they'd be sent to the penitentiary in Yuma."

"And did this meeting take place between the two families?"

"Sure did. Both the Taylor and the Condon men and older boys—those that were still alive—came into town armed to the teeth. I told Bradford that he might as well send two runaway trains hurtling down a track at each other because the meeting was going to be a terrible wreck, but he wouldn't believe it. Bradford foolishly believed he had the skills and authority to finally put the feud to rest."

"But he was sadly mistaken."

"I'm afraid so," Cynthia said. "I was there against my family's wishes, and had a rifle ready to kill the first man that tried to shoot Bradford down. But I needn't have worried. As soon as the two sides came together, they went at each other with guns and knives. It was a real war with blood and bullets flying in all directions."

"How badly was Mr. Gumm wounded?"

"Very badly. But he managed to get out of the middle of that shootout and I got him to our ranch, where he spent months recuperating. For a while we didn't even know if he was going to pull through. Bradford should have died of his wounds, but he has a very strong constitution for an Easterner."

"And then what happened?"

Cynthia took a deep breath. "One night some of the Taylor men showed up and wanted to speak to Bradford. They told him that he *had* to take their side in the feud or they'd shoot him on sight."

"And what did he say?" Longarm asked.

Cynthia smiled a little sadly. "I was proud of him because he refused to take their side of the affair against the sheep men. So the Taylors rode off vowing to kill him the next time they met. And guess what happened less than a week later?"

"I think I can guess," Longarm said.

"Yes, I'll just bet you can. The Condon men appeared at sundown with their sheepdogs. I can smell sheep and the Condon men a half mile downwind. They're a rough, illiterate bunch, but they're no worse than the Taylor family, who are consumed by their greed for land and cattle."

Longarm took another sip of his whiskey. "So the sheep men also insisted that Bradford take their side on the feud."

"Exactly," Cynthia told him. "And of course Bradford refused. He told them that he was a federal officer of the law and that the feud had gone on so long and had taken so many lives that it no longer mattered who started the fight. All Bradford wanted was to make a lasting peace."

"And the Condon men answered?"

"They said there could *never* be a peace. Too many of their men and boys had been ambushed. A blood debt had to be settled and it wouldn't happen until the last Taylor man was pushing up dirt."

"Did they also threaten to kill Bradford the next time they came across him?"

"No." Cynthia shook her head. "Actually, they wanted to kill Bradford right there in front of our ranch house. But we wouldn't allow that, so they rode away madder than hell. My father got angry at Bradford and told him he was causing us big trouble, and that he'd have to leave as soon as he was able to ride a horse."

Longarm wasn't pleased by this news. "So that means that he's not at your ranch any longer."

"He left about three days later," Cynthia said. "And I'm not sure where Bradford went. He was healing, but not at full strength. And when I told him that he and I would never be happy together, he decided to leave our part of the country."

Longarm felt supreme disappointment. "Well, isn't that a fine mess of hash? I've got his fiancée in tow and I'm supposed to find Bradford and return him to safety. Now you're telling me that he isn't even around anymore."

"I'm sorry, Custis. We did what we could for Bradford, but he'd have been ambushed had he stayed in Pine Valley."

"So where do you think he might have gone?"

Cynthia thought about that a moment, then said, "If I had to guess, I'd say he might have gone down to the Apache country."

Again, this was not what Longarm had hoped to hear. "What the hell for?"

"To get dead or to get famous. That's the way that Bradford is and he's not going to change."

Longarm drained his glass and clenched his jaw. "I've got better things to do with my life than be running around with a Miss Konrad whom I don't even like. And it gets even worse given the fact that she has me chasing a man who she thinks loves her, but now I learn doesn't."

"Yeah," Cynthia said, "it does sound like you've got your tit in a wringer and there's no wiggle room." She looked down at his empty glass and then her own. "Despite everything, I think we have a lot in common."

Longarm couldn't think of a single thing that he had in common with this ranch girl. "Like what?"

She refilled their glasses. "Well, for starters, it's obvious that we both like this brand of whiskey."

He knew she was trying to raise his sunken spirits and smiled. "Yeah, that we do."

"And also we've both been caused a big headache by Bradford G. Gumm."

"True enough," he admitted. "Although your headache is past and mine is only going to grow worse."

"That's not exactly true," she told him. "My family is also now in the hot soup. You have to understand that, before Bradford, my family was on civil terms with both the Taylors and the Condons. Now, both families are mad as hell at us and they're not the kind of people who let slights or grudges pass without trying to get even."

Longarm nodded and realized he was feeling a little

drunk. Cynthia could handle her liquor awfully well for a woman, and he couldn't help but wonder how it would be to bed her tonight.

"What are you smiling about?" she asked, cocking her head to one side and squinting through one eye.

"Nothing."

"Are you thinking what *I* think you're thinking?"

Longarm shrugged trying to look innocent. "I was just reflecting on how you are one hell of a fine-looking woman. How come you didn't get married about ten years ago?"

"I did." Her expression changed. "My husband was a cowboy and he was killed in a stampede."

"I'm sorry to hear that."

"Me, too. We were very much in love and he was a fine man."

"Did you have any kids?"

"Nope." She took a long swallow. "My late husband and I both liked horses, dogs, and cattle a lot better than kids. If I'd had a baby, I'd probably have given it away to someone I thought would make it a good mother."

"At least you're honest about it."

Cynthia looked him straight in the eye. "I'm *always* honest."

"I believe that. So tell me why you came up here to Flagstaff."

"I knew that Miss Konrad was on her way and I wanted to try and tell her that she was making a big mistake by chasing after a man that really never loved her."

"So are you going to tell her that first thing tomorrow morning?" Longarm asked.

"I'm not sure, but I don't think so."

"If you came all this way, then why not?"

"Because," Cynthia explained, "Miss Konrad wouldn't

believe me. And she'd know that we'd probably been lovers and think that it was Bradford who left me. Then I expect that she would decide I was just trying to chase her off so that I could get her man. Do you think a rich and beautiful woman like Julia Konrad could believe a simple Arizona ranch girl like me would jilt a man like Bradford G. Gumm?"

"No," Longarm admitted, "I don't."

"Of course she wouldn't! Custis, the way I see it is that you have to figure out some way to get that woman to go back to wherever she came from. Just turn around and both of you get back on the train and head for Denver."

"That's impossible," Longarm said. "I have orders to put a stop to the range war. And as for Julia Konrad, she'd never go back without finding Bradford and getting some answers."

"She won't get the answers she's looking for," Cynthia warned.

"I know that. Julia is arrogant and loves attention. She has no business being out here and might get me killed, but I still have to admire her determination. Despite how she may appear on the outside, Julia is tough as nails. I suspect you and she have at least that much in common."

Cynthia looked down for a moment, and then she looked up at Longarm. "Have you already made love to her?"

The question caught Longarm completely off guard. "What the hell makes you think that?"

"You're a man who loves to love women and Miss Konrad is quite a beauty."

"She's not even close to being my type."

Cynthia placed her glass down and leaned close. "Am *I* your type?"

Had he been completely sober Longarm might have run the other way. After all, one independent and headstrong woman was more than enough to handle and now he was facing a second.

"Look, Cynthia," he began as he chose his words very carefully, "I'm leaving in the morning with Miss Konrad. She's paying for a team of horses and a buggy."

"So what?"

"So I have to be focused on taking care of her, myself, and trying to figure out how to tell her that Bradford is not what she thinks he is . . . or was."

"You've got a load of trouble on your mind," Cynthia said, her face and lips almost touching his face and lips. "That's plain to see. But what I think you need is a loyal and loving partner."

"I don't need a partner," he whispered.

She began to unbutton her blouse, and Longarm could feel his temperature rising. "I'm going to try and change your mind."

"Cynthia, I . . ."

She shushed him with her lips and the next thing Longarm knew they were on her bed and tearing off every last shred of clothing.

To hell with it, Longarm thought. *I'm up against more than I can handle so I might as well give in and enjoy her ride.*

Chapter 9

Longarm and Cynthia were locked in the throes of sweaty passion when there was a loud knock on the door.

Longarm tried to ignore the sound and kept pumping, but the hammering only grew louder and more insistent.

"Do you have a gun?" Cynthia panted as she lay under him with her long legs wrapped tightly around his waist.

"Yes," he grunted.

"Then grab it and shoot whoever is there. Shoot right through the door and kill 'em quick!"

"I'd better not do that," Longarm rasped as he pounded his seed into the woman while groaning with pleasure.

"Then get off me if you're finished and *I'll* kill 'em!"

Cynthia rolled an exhausted Longarm off her and reached for his gun. There was a look on her pretty face that said she wasn't bluffing, so Longarm decided he'd better grab the cowgirl before she actually did kill whoever was pounding on the door.

"Marshal, are you in there!" the voice called. "Come on out! We need to talk!"

"Julia?" he asked, recognizing her strained voice.

"Of course it's me! Open up. What are you doing in

there? The desk clerk said you were given Room Seven for the night, but this is Room Ten. What's going on?"

"Get rid of her," Cynthia hissed, "because I'm not half-finished with you yet."

Longarm removed her hand from the butt of his gun and kissed Cynthia. "I'll get rid of her."

He grabbed his pants and walked barefoot to the door, which he opened a crack.

"Marshal Long, I forgot to ask you about—"

"Julia, it can wait until morning."

"No, it can't!"

"But I'm real busy at the moment," he said, realizing that he was sweating and there was a big and all too obvious tent pole rearing up in the front of his pants.

Julia managed to sneak a peek past Longarm and when she saw the naked cowgirl, she shrieked and threw her shoulder into the door crying, "Who is *that!*"

Longarm stuck his foot in the door to keep it from opening, but the bottom of the door crushed his toes and he let out a whoop. Losing his balance, he nearly fell over as Julia pushed her way into the room.

"Who are *you!*" Julia demanded, eyes stabbing like daggers into the naked Cynthia.

Cynthia didn't bother to cover herself. Instead, she jumped up from the bed with Longarm's seed running down her thighs and shouted, "I'm the woman that your so-called fiancé wanted to marry instead of marrying *you.*"

Longarm saw something very much akin to horror and madness leap into Julia's eyes, and then the woman from the East attacked Cynthia like an enraged lioness. The next thing Longarm knew they were both on the floor clawing, spitting, biting, and flailing at each other. Cynthia was naked and that was to her disadvantage, but she was tougher, and soon was on top of the socialite with her clenched fists flying.

"Hey!" Longarm shouted, pulling the Arizona wildcat off Julia and dragging her kicking and hissing to the other side of the room. "Just stop it, both of you!"

One of Julia's eyes was already swelling and there was blood on her lips, but Cynthia had deep scratch marks on one of her breasts and a bloody nose. Longarm doubted he had ever seen two women who looked more ready to kill each other.

"Custis, I want her out of your room!" Julia screamed.

"This isn't *his* room, you crazy bitch, this is *my* room!"

For the first time since Longarm had known Julia, the woman was absolutely speechless. Then she whirled on Longarm and her eyes dropped to the bulge in his pants and her lips curled back with contempt. "You couldn't even wait until we found my Bradford? You had to get some whore up here and get laid before we left?"

"Whore! You called me a whore?" Cynthia screeched, launching herself at Julia with maniacal fury.

It was all that Longarm could do to keep the two bloodied women apart, and he took a couple of wild punches in the process. "Stop it, dammit!"

They finally paused and Longarm said, "Julia, I do have Room Seven, but I got a little sidetracked."

"That's a fine way of putting it!"

"Go back to your own room and I'll see you in the morning."

"I don't think so," Julia spit. "I don't think that I want to ever see you again, Marshal. I can and will find Bradford all on my own."

"Don't be ridiculous."

"I'm not being ridiculous," she snapped. "I'm being

truthful. I thought you were a man with some integrity, but that's obviously my mistake. So I'll hire someone that I can stand the sight of tomorrow to take me down to Pine Valley. I don't need you."

Cynthia said, "You're even stupider than I thought, Miss Konrad. Because you see, Bradford isn't in Pine Valley anymore. He's gone and very well might be dead by now, but you'll never know because you'll never find him. All you'll find in Pine Valley is death, deceit, and trouble you can't even begin to handle alone."

"Who are you?" Julia demanded.

Cynthia gave her name and then added, "Bradford and I were lovers soon after he came to Pine Valley."

"Liar!"

"Liar, huh? Well, if that's true, then how do I know that your Bradford has a big mole on his—"

"Stop it!" Julia screamed. "I don't want to hear about it!"

Longarm realized that Julia knew where the mole was just as surely as Cynthia. For a moment there was an awkward silence, and then Longarm pushed Julia out of the room saying, "Meet me for breakfast down in the hotel lobby. We all need to calm down and put our heads together if we want to be of any help to Bradford."

Julia's lips curled down at the corners with unconcealed contempt. "Marshal Long, you are a totally despicable lawman, but perhaps you're right. I just don't ever want to see that . . . that woman again."

"Same for me!" Cynthia shouted, jabbing a forefinger at Julia and shaking with fury. "No wonder Bradford was trying so hard to get away from you back East."

Julia slammed the door and stomped down the hallway while Longarm went over to the bed and threw down a big swallow of whiskey. He shook his head and moaned, "This is the most screwed-up situation I've ever been in during all the years that I've worn a badge. For two damn cents I'd toss my badge out your window, leave Arizona, and let you two women kill each other."

Cynthia sat down beside him with a handkerchief to her bloody nose. "I can understand that. Really, I can. What did you think of the fight? I really beat the crap out of Miss High-and-Mighty, didn't I!"

"Yeah," he said, "you did. But she got in a few good licks herself. Is your nose broken?"

"Hell, no." Cynthia looked down at the claw marks on her right breast. "That bitch has fingernails sharper than the claws of a wildcat. I wish you'd have let me shoot her when she first started beating on my door."

"No, you don't," Longarm said.

"Sure I do!" Cynthia studied the blood on her handkerchief and then frowned. "I think our fun time is over for tonight. But maybe we can do better tomorrow night."

"There won't be a tomorrow night," Longarm said with absolute certainty.

"Sure there will be. You're still bringing that crazy bitch down to Pine Valley, aren't you?"

"I don't think she wants to be around me anymore."

"That's because she is carrying a secret torch for you, Custis."

"Oh, bullshit."

"No, it's true! Why else would she go so far off the deep end just because we were in here screwing? Only one reason, and that is that she considers you her second man."

"You shouldn't have told her that you and Bradford were lovers and that he wanted to leave her."

"Why not?" Cynthia asked. "It's the truth."

"Maybe so, but it wasn't a bit kind."

"What has kindness to do with a man who is supposed to be in love with you and says he wants to marry you, but is secretly trying to get as far from you as he can?"

Longarm shook his head. "I've had enough to drink and I need some sleep. I'm going back to my own room and just pretend that this was a nightmare and that it will all be gone tomorrow."

"It won't be," Cynthia promised. "Because in the morning when you see that woman for breakfast, she is going to bite your head off. We both know that she will, so why don't you tell her to get on her broom and go back to wherever it is she came from."

"And then what?"

"You and I will go find Bradford."

"Oh, no!" Longarm threw up both hands in protest. "I've had all the woman trouble I need with Julia Konrad, and I'm not about to have deal with you next."

"I can take you to unknown places that you would never find alone," she said. "I know how to speak sign with the Apache and they trust me, but they'll never trust you. If Bradford went in among them, you'll need my help or all you'll get is scalped."

"I still have to go to Pine Valley and put a stop to that range war," he said, realizing he had an awful headache.

Cynthia just shrugged her bare shoulders. "I can help ease you into that feud as well. You better face up to it before I lose patience with you, Custis. You need me."

"So you keep saying."

"And," she added, "I was enjoying your body before that witch broke up our party. You got yours, but I didn't quite get to where I need to go."

"You could find a lot of men to help you do that."

"Uh-uh," she said. "I am real picky and I picked *you*."

The pain in Longarm's head was intensifying and he needed to get away by himself and get some sleep.

"We'll talk about it in the morning," he hedged.

"Before or after you talk to that witch?"

"I don't know."

"It had better be afterward," Cynthia decided. "I'll want to know what she's going to do about finding Bradford before I make my own plan to help you find him."

"Whatever," Longarm said as he pulled on his boots and staggered to the door. "Just don't wake me up early."

"I'm a cowgirl and I always get up with the roosters," Cynthia announced. "But I'll be merciful and allow you a few extra hours of sleep. You're going to need to be strong and awake when you face that rich bitch for breakfast."

Longarm was sure that was true. But he was also sure that if he could somehow extract himself from this whole mess, he would do it in less than a heartbeat.

Chapter 10

Longarm was fast asleep when Cynthia started banging on his door and yelling for him to wake up. He took a deep breath and knuckled sleep and a slight hangover from his eyes.

"What time is it!" he yelled from the bed.

"It's nine o'clock. I've been up for three hours and you're supposed to meet that Konrad woman for breakfast, only she hasn't shown up yet, either."

"She's probably sleeping in just like I was," Longarm said, wishing he could get another hour or two of shut-eye before he had to face Julia. "Go . . . go find something to do for a while."

There was a long silence, and then Cynthia said, "I don't think Miss Konrad is even in town anymore."

Longarm sat bolt upright. He grabbed his pants and yanked them on as he stumbled to the door. Opening it, he saw Cynthia smiling, even though the cowgirl's nose was swollen and her eye sockets slightly discolored.

"What did you say?" Longarm asked, hoping he'd misunderstood.

"I said that I think Miss Rich Bitch done flew the coop. Blew this town. Headed out to the great unknown."

Longarm grabbed Cynthia and dragged her into his room, then shut the door. She laughed and poked him playfully. "Are you lookin' for a little lovin' this morning, Marshal?"

"No!" He lowered his voice. "Why did you say you think Julia has left town?"

"Because the desk clerk told me she did late last night. Left with two men and they were all in a helluva big hurry."

Longarm swore silently and began to get fully dressed. "What time did she leave and did the desk clerk recognize the men she was with?"

"She left about two o'clock this morning and he didn't recognize either man. Said they were strangers and didn't say a word. Each one had Miss Konrad by an arm and they were moving real fast across the lobby. The night clerk said he mostly just saw their backs on their way out the door."

"Maybe he mistook Julia for some other woman," Longarm said, desperately hoping this was the case. "I can't imagine who she'd have been with at that hour or why she'd have left."

"Remember that she was sure was hopping mad at us."

Longarm buckled on his gun belt. "I know that, but Julia's no fool and she understood that she needed me to take her to Pine Valley."

"Maybe she found someone to take her there that she liked a whole lot better'n you," Cynthia replied. "And maybe those two men knew where to find Bradford . . . or at least convinced her they did."

"But why would they do that?"

Cynthia gave him a deprecating look and said, "Come on, you of all people ought to be able to figure that one out.

The woman is rich and beautiful. They don't care about the fact that she's also got the temperament of a dirt badger. They'll rape and then ransom her for all she's worth."

"We don't know that. They might have been honest men."

"Sure," Cynthia said cryptically. "And that's why they were giving her the bum's rush at two o'clock this morning. Was she carrying any cash?"

"A thousand or so, I suppose."

"That's a fortune. I also saw her jewelry, and what she had was worth a mint. Custis, don't you realize that, to a couple of hard, broke men, Julia Konrad would seem better than striking a vein of pure gold?"

Longarm knew that Cynthia was right as he hurried outside and went down to Julia's room, where he hammered on her door until a sleepy guest in a nearby room shouted for him to knock it off.

"Try the knob?" Cynthia suggested.

Longarm turned the knob, and was amazed that the door was unlocked. He threw the door open and burst inside. It only took a glance to see that Julia was gone and that she had not taken any of her luggage.

Longarm dashed out of the room and downstairs to the hotel lobby, where he found the clerk. "Tell me about Miss Konrad leaving last night!"

"I don't know anything about that because I didn't come to work until eight o'clock this morning. I do know that she still hasn't paid her room bill."

"Who was on shift at two o'clock this morning and where can I find him?"

"Homer was on last night, same as always. He works for a free room here at the hotel, his meals, and a little pay."

"What's his room number?"

The desk clerk hesitated. "Now wait a minute. Homer was up all night and he doesn't want to be awakened."

Longarm reached across the hotel desk and grabbed the man by the front of his shirt. "This is an emergency! Tell me his room number before I shake you like a rat!"

"Room Twenty-seven!" the man cried.

Longarm released him and went tearing back upstairs.

He slammed his fist into the door of room so hard, it nearly tore off its hinges. "Homer, this is Marshal Long. Open up! I have to talk to you."

"Go away!"

Longarm supposed that he should have run back downstairs and gotten the key to this room from the current desk clerk, but he just wasn't in the mood to be denied, so he threw his shoulder to the door and sent it flying open.

Homer was trying to go back to sleep, but that all changed when Longarm burst inside with Cynthia right on his heels.

"What the hell is goin' on!" Homer cried, sitting up in a red flannel undershirt.

"I need to know who took Miss Julia Konrad out of the hotel this morning at two o'clock."

Bill knuckled his eyes. "I never saw 'em before. They were strangers and I didn't even have time to see their faces because they were scootin' across the lobby so fast."

"Did you see Miss Konrad's face?"

"As a matter of fact, she did turn and glance back at me over her shoulder."

Longarm moved closer. "And how did she look?"

"What do you mean?" Homer asked with obvious confusion.

"Did she look scared? Excited. What?"

Homer yawned and scratched his face. "I dunno. She looked as pretty as ever. But it was two o'clock and she also looked tired. Kinda strained."

"And she didn't say anything?"

"Not a word." Homer wrung his long nose. "But now that I think about it, she did try to say something, but one of the men that was pushin' her along kinda gave her a hard tug and then she was gone out the door."

Longarm couldn't think of another thing to ask the night clerk. The man hadn't seen the faces of the ones that had taken Julia, and so he wouldn't be able to identify them if they were still in Flagstaff. And even worse was the fact that Longarm couldn't really be sure if Julia was taken by force or by choice. But if he had to choose one or the other, he would have to choose by force.

"Marshal, I'm sorry that I can't help you anymore. You broke the door latch and I'll have to see that it gets fixed today. But right now I sure would like to go back to sleep. I got to go on shift tonight same as usual and I need some rest."

"Sorry about the door and the interruption, Homer."

Longarm closed the door and turned to Cynthia. "I'd better start asking around to see if anyone else saw them leave."

"That is doubtful."

"Someone might have seen something," Longarm said hopefully. "As it stands right now, I don't know why they took her, much less *where* they took her."

"My guess is that they might still be in town."

"And why do you say that?" Longarm asked.

"Because if they want to rape her, why go far? And if they took her for ransom, they'll need to find a way to contact whoever it is that can send the ransom money. That means that they'll need a telegraph office. Writing a letter is too slow and unreliable. They might also try to take her back East by train."

"I don't think so," Longarm said. "Julia Konrad stands out in any crowd and she'd be recognized."

"Good point," Cynthia conceded.

Longarm's mind was starting to race. "What's the nearest town from here that has a telegraph office?"

"That would be Williams about forty miles east."

"What's it like?"

"Tough railroad and logging town. You've already seen a thousand of 'em."

"Does Williams have a town marshal?" Longarm asked.

"Nope. Last one hired got shot and they couldn't get another fool to take his place."

Longarm thought a moment and said, "I'll start asking around and, if I don't get any leads, then I'll go to Williams."

"I got a horse and can get you one to rent."

"Thanks for the offer," Longarm said. "But now I better get busy asking questions. If Julia is still in this town, then I need to find her right away."

"That rich bitch is as loud as a foghorn in a funeral parlor. Those two men might just get fed up with and shoot her, then walk away cold."

"I don't think so," Longarm said. "There is way too much money to be gained."

"They'll earn every penny of it," Cynthia countered.

Longarm thought the woman was probably right, but he didn't tell her so.

Chapter 11

Longarm spent most of the morning asking everyone he could find if they had seen Julia Konrad the night before, and it wasn't until almost noon that one of Flagstaff's drunks came up to him and said, "I hear you been askin' about that rich lady."

"That's right."

"I seen her leave last night."

The man's eyes were red and bloodshot, his clothing worn and dirty. He might have been forty, but was probably much younger, and he stank so bad it would be easy to think he had just climbed out of a pigpen, and maybe he had. He tried to hold Longarm's gaze, but failed.

Longarm knew that the only reason the man was standing before him was that he hoped to get a few dollars in return for his questionable information.

"Where did you see the lady?"

"Well," the drunk stammered, hands shaking noticeably, "I saw her come out of your hotel early this morning with two men."

"And what did the men look like?"

The drunk wiped his mouth and swallowed hard. "I could sure use a drink, Marshal. It would help me remember."

Longarm's first impulse was to tell the drunk to go away. But since he had no other witnesses or leads, he decided to play along for a few more minutes and said, "I might buy you a drink if you can convince me that you really did see Miss Konrad leaving the hotel. So tell me something I haven't already heard from the desk clerk."

"Well," the man began, "I still say I could remember a lot better with a drink. Just a shot of whiskey to clear my mind and throat."

Longarm reached into his pocket and gave the drunk four bits. His eyes softened and he started to leave, but Longarm grabbed him by the collar. "That will buy you a couple of drinks, mister. But if you really did see Miss Konrad leave and can give me some true information, then I'll give you a silver dollar and you can buy a full bottle of rotgut."

"I watched 'em leave the hotel, all right," the drunk said quietly. "The two men were big and they had a buckboard filled to overflowing with straw waiting."

"Straw?"

"That's what it looked like to me. Might have been grass hay, but I'm pretty sure it was straw like you'd put down in a stall. Gawd knows I've pitchforked enough straw in my life to know it when I see it."

"I did see some straw in the street outside the hotel," Longarm said, more to himself than to the drunk.

"Well, they put her up between 'em in that buckboard and they headed out of town."

"Going in which direction?"

"South."

"Are you sure?"

98

"Yes, sir!" The drunk wet his cracked lips. "Now do I get that silver dollar?"

"Just another question or two. Can you describe these men?"

"It was dark out, but I seen their faces in the street lamps. They were big and both wore full beards."

"Tall men?"

He shook his head. "Not so tall as just big. Strong-lookin'. They wore guns and bandannas around their necks and their buckboard was pulled by two horses. Sorrels, I'd say."

"Had you ever seen either one before?"

"No, sir."

Longarm took a silver dollar out of his pocket, but he didn't give it to the drunk quite yet. "I want you to walk with me out to the south of town. If I see straw, even a single shred of it, then I'll give you the dollar. But if not, then you've gotten all the money from me that you're going to get from me."

Disappointment clouded the man's ruined face. "Marshal, couldn't I just go into the saloon and have one drink before we go lookin'?"

"Nope," Longarm said, grabbing the man by the collar. "Miss Konrad's life might be in danger and I can't waste the time waiting for you to have a drink."

"Listen, I drink *real* fast."

"I'll bet you do, but we're going for a little walk first."

The drunk wasn't the least bit happy, but he nodded and started up the street, and when they got to the Hotel Monte Vista, he bent and picked up some straw. It had already been trampled in the dirt. "See, I told you."

"Let's go on and see if we can find more straw."

Longarm was walking faster than the drunk, and he was

finding wisps of straw here and there on the street, all of it trampled by horses and wagons, but all of it looking fresh.

"How far we got to follow this damned old straw?" the drunk whined when they got to the south edge of town.

Longarm's eyes raced ahead, and the straw was more evident as the traffic had thinned on the southbound road.

"I've seen enough," he said, giving the man a silver dollar. "Anything else you can tell me that might help in my search?"

"Nope. Good luck!"

The drunk was already shuffling off quickly toward the nearest saloon. Longarm took a moment to watch the man, and then he headed back to town. Cynthia was waiting for him when he entered the hotel lobby, and he took her by the arm and led her over to a place where they would not be overheard. "Did you mean what you said about getting us horses?"

"I have my own horse boarded at the livery and I can get you one to ride for a price."

"Then do it," he said. "I think that the men that took Julia last night are traveling south in a buckboard filled with straw."

"Why would they be haulin' a lot of straw?"

"Maybe they planned to tie her up and then cover her with it this morning at first light so that no one would see Julia being abducted."

"That would be smart. Who saw her being taken away this morning?"

"Just a drunk that was probably prowling around looking for someone to steal money off," Longarm answered. "At any rate, we need to get those horses and follow a trail of straw."

"If that's what you want to do, then we'll do 'er," Cynthia said. "You got any money to pay the livery owner for the use of his horse?"

Longarm gave Cynthia four dollars.

She frowned. "I can't get you much of a horse for four dollars."

He gave her another dollar. "We'll need some supplies, too," he said. "I'll go buy them and meet you here in front of the hotel in a half hour."

"Make it forty-five minutes," Cynthia told him. "South, you say?"

"That's right."

"Then I'll be headed home," she said as she hurried off. Then she called over her shoulder. "Maybe we'll go to my daddy's ranch and I'll introduce you to him and my brothers. You might decide that ranching beats squiring spoiled women around and decide to stay."

"I don't think so. Go on now and hurry along."

Cynthia made a face at him.

Longarm went up to his hotel room and gathered his things, then paid the desk clerk on the way out. "What about what Miss Konrad owes for her room?" the man asked.

"I'm going to have to find and ask her about that," Longarm promised, "just as soon as I can."

The desk clerk didn't look too hopeful, but Longarm didn't care as he left on the run. He trotted over to the dry-goods store and bought provisions in addition to some extra ammunition. After all, he was going to Pine Valley and there was a range war going on whether or not he found Julia.

If he could find her soon enough, then she might be yet saved. If not, then her death was on his shoulders and there would be hell to pay when and *if* he ever got back to the office in Denver.

Chapter 12

Longarm stared at the rental horse with disapproval. It was a jug-headed gray gelding with prominent hip bones and a U-shaped neck. Mostly the animal was white, but it had been in so many fights and skirmishes that there were black hair slashes throughout its thick coat. It had very large feet and crooked front legs.

"Is this really the best that you could do for five dollars?" he asked Cynthia.

"Actually, the livery owner wanted ten dollars to rent the horse, so I bought him outright along with the saddle, bridle, and blanket."

"Whatever you paid, it was too much," Longarm said, noting that the saddle was worn.

Cynthia just snorted. "I know this gray horse isn't handsome like *you*, Marshal, but I just happen to also know the cowboy that sold this horse and he always told me that the animal is sound and surefooted. He's also fast and has a lot of bottom, meaning endurance."

"Is he a bucker or a biter?"

"Nope. But he does have a rough gait. *Real* rough. The

cowboy that sold him said this gray trots and gallops so hard that it gave him hemorrhoids."

"Oh, swell."

Cynthia brushed his concern off as casually as she would a pesky fly. "You just need to stand up in the stirrups when we're trotting or galloping and you'll be fine."

"The saddle is pretty bad as well," Longarm groused as he tossed a canvas sack with the provisions he'd bought behind the cantle and tied it down with the strings.

"You're sure a big complainer," Cynthia noted.

Longarm jammed his boot in the stirrup and swung on board. The stirrups were much too short, but he was in a hurry to get after Julia, so he didn't bother to step back down to make adjustments.

"You gonna ride with your knees all bent like that?"

"Until we need to stop and rest."

"That might not be for a while, Marshal."

"Let's go!" he said, cradling his rifle across the front of the saddle and giving the gray a kick with his heels.

The gray horse shot forward so abruptly that Longarm damn near spilled over the back of the animal. He had to make a desperate grab for his saddle horn, and in doing so he dropped the Winchester.

Cynthia owned a pretty buckskin mare, and now she dismounted and collected the rifle. Handing it up to him, she said, "You aren't much of a horseman, are you."

"I can ride the longest, hardest trail," Longarm replied defensively. "The fact that I can't rope a steer or ride like a Comanche doesn't bother me."

"I never saw a Comanche ride," she said. "I have seen some Apache that could ride bareback like they were part of their pony, but I never saw a Comanche horseman."

"Mount up and let's go," Longarm told the woman.

104

Cynthia scowled. "One thing you need to know is that I don't take well to being ordered around. Not by any man."

"I'll try to keep it in mind," he said, taking the edge out of his voice. "And I didn't mean to bark at you. It's just that I'm worried about Miss Konrad and I don't want to waste any more time. Those men who took her already have a good eight-hour head start."

"Sure, but they're in a buckboard filled with straw and we're on horseback, so we ought to overtake 'em by nightfall . . . if you don't get tossed and hurt."

Longarm bit his tongue and this time gently put his heels to the ugly gray horse, which took off at a trot so jarring that he had to grit his teeth to keep them from clicking.

They rode for three awful hours following the trail of straw, which did not desert them. By then Longarm was in more than a little pain. Because he hadn't, taken the time to lengthen his stirrups and because they'd pushed a fast pace, the insides of his knees were already starting to chafe and blister. Also, given that his mount was so rough to ride, his back felt like a branch ready to splinter.

"Stop!" he called.

"What's the matter?" Cynthia asked.

"I've got to take a rest."

"The trail is pretty fresh now," Cynthia told him while glancing up at the sun. "We've only got about three more hours of daylight and I'd hate to lose 'em in the dark."

"Me, too," Longarm agreed, "but if we don't stop so that I can rest and readjust these stirrups, then I won't be worth a damn when we do overtake the buckboard."

"All right."

They dismounted, and it was all that Longarm could do to stand as he lengthened the stirrups and drank from his new canteen. While he was doing this, Cynthia hiked up through a stand of ponderosa to a low rise of land and studied the horizon before them. Longarm collapsed on the ground and closed his eyes feeling pure pain.

"How's the saddle sores coming?" Cynthia asked with a caring smile when she returned a half hour later.

"They're doing just fine," Longarm answered. "I'm the one that is having a hell of a hard time."

"Let me pull down your pants and take a look at what is causing your misery."

Longarm unbuckled his belt and pulled his pants down. Even he was surprised at how red the inflammation was inside his legs.

"Damnation!" Cynthia said. "We should have stopped a long time ago and fixed your stirrups. Lucky thing for you that I have some hog fat in my saddlebags to grease your legs up real good."

"Hog fat?" Longarm shook his head. "Damned if I want you to lather my legs up with hog fat."

"It's not only fat, but some other liniment mixed in, and it'll help keep your skin from tearing off and getting infected. I promise you'll feel better with some of this hog-fat liniment rubbed on."

"Okay," Longarm told her. "But I'm not sure that I can ride another mile on that gray horse."

"We'll switch saddles and you can ride my buckskin mare," Cynthia suggested. "It'll only take a minute, and the mare has a trot that feels like you're in a rocking chair."

"You talked me into it," he said as she got the hog fat and then liberally applied it to the insides of his inflamed legs. She winked and said, "Maybe I ought to lather up your balls and Big Billy so you can use 'em on me one of these nights when we are together."

106

The suggestion was so ludicrous that Longarm had to laugh, which was exactly what the woman had hoped for.

"All right," she said, uncinching their saddles and making the swap. "Time for you to climb on board my Lula Bell and we get to moving again."

Longarm eased himself back into the saddle and it still hurt plenty, but was bearable.

"Here is your rifle. Don't drop it this time."

Longarm ignored the insulting remark. Cynthia's buckskin was shorter than the ugly gray, and he knew at once that the mare was easy to ride when they set off after the buckboard.

"By the way," Longarm said, "did you see anything from up on that rise of land?"

"Yep." She said nothing more, but kept riding. Because the gray gelding was so tall, Cynthia and he were about on the same eye level.

"Well?" Longarm replied impatiently. "Are you going to tell me what you saw?"

"I saw the buckboard. At least I think I did. It's still about three miles up ahead. But I'm sure it's the one we're after."

Longarm instantly forgot about his aches and pains.

"Maybe," he said, judging the risks, "you ought to hold back and let me go on ahead alone."

"And maybe," she countered, "you ought to keep your mouth shut and let me help you out. Do you have a plan?"

Longarm raised his rifle and flexed his arm muscles. "I'd like to try to get ahead of them rather than come riding up from behind. If we can get up in front, we can lay a trap and catch them by surprise."

"You hope."

"It's our best chance," Longarm told her. "Have we got enough daylight to do it?"

"I'd say that, if we pushed it hard for the next hour, we can get up ahead of 'em."

Longarm sure didn't want to "push it hard," but Cynthia had been right about everything so far, so he nodded. "Then let's do it."

They set off at a gallop and although it hurt, the hog fat and whatever else was in the grease seemed to have a powerful, soothing effect and so the galloping was bearable. Now and then Longarm glanced over at Cynthia on the ugly gray horse, and she didn't seem to be bouncing even a little. In fact, she appeared to be joined as one with the rough-riding gelding.

Sometimes a man just had to admit that a woman could do things a whole lot better than he could. He just hoped that Cynthia could shoot as well as she could ride if and when it came down to swapping bullets with Julia's abductors.

Chapter 13

"Here they come!" Longarm whispered, levering a shell into his rifle. "Now remember what we agreed to. The last thing I need is for two dead or shot women on my conscience."

"I'll stay out of sight unless you need me," she promised. "But don't take any unnecessary chances."

"I'll do whatever it takes to get Julia back unharmed," Longarm vowed.

"Just remember, Marshal, you can't do that *dead*. These boys are hard and fast on the trigger."

The buckboard was only about a quarter of a mile up the forest road, and as Longarm peered from behind a big ponderosa, he could see that both men were large with black beards. "Cynthia, do you recognize them?"

She squinted and studied the men closely. "I believe that I do."

"Who are they?"

"They're Taylor men. Cousins Rafe and Gaspar."

"They're on the cattlemen side of the range war?"

"Right up to their necks," Cynthia told him. "And I'll tell you something else . . . either one of them can shoot the eye out of a sparrow on the wing, so don't you be taking any chances."

"I won't," Longarm promised. "Just stay out of sight and let me handle this like I have many times in the past."

"I'm going to be invisible," she promised. "Unless they try to kill you."

Longarm wore his six-gun on his left hip, butt forward. He eased it up and down in his holster, and then flexed his fingers as he gripped the Winchester. He would try to get these Taylor men to throw their hands up, but if they went for their weapons, he would shoot them without an instant's hesitation.

"Here goes," he said, taking a deep breath as the buckboard came nearer with no Julia Konrad in sight, although he thought he saw a mound under the straw. "Let's hope these boys are smarter than they look."

"They aren't," Cynthia said in a terse voice. "Count on it."

Longarm jumped out from behind the big yellow-barked ponderosa pine and threw the rifle to his shoulder yelling, "Rein up and reach for the sky!"

The Taylor men didn't do either, but instead went for their side arms.

"Damn," Longarm swore as he aimed and fired a bullet into the driver's chest knocking him back on his seat.

The second big man already had his pistol up, and Longarm didn't hesitate as he shot to kill. His rifle kicked hard at his shoulder and the man took a slug and hollered like a bull elk in rutting season.

"Drop that gun!" Longarm ordered. "Or I'll put my next bullet right through that thick skull of yours!"

The man dropped his gun and slumped forward as the two horses pulling the buckboard bolted. Longarm sprinted forward trying to grab the fallen reins, but he wasn't successful and the buckboard went flying past him up the rutted forest road. The first man he'd shot bounced off his seat, and the second man he'd probably mortally wounded soon also toppled off the buckboard and struck the ground rolling.

"Cynthia!" Longarm shouted. "We've got to get to that wagon before it overturns and kills Julia!"

Cynthia jumped up and swung onto her buckskin mare. She swept past Longarm and went barreling down the road after the buckboard. She was riding Longarm's livery saddle and the stirrups were out of her reach, but that didn't seem to hinder her in the slightest. Longarm briefly considered joining the chase, but he knew that Cynthia was well able to run down the buckboard before he could be of help on the gray gelding, so he hurried to the first man and knew at once that he was dead.

"Shit!" Longarm swore as he dropped his rifle and trotted up the road to the second man, who was trying to crawl into the forest while leaving a trail of blood. The man must have heard Longarm's pounding boots on the road because he rolled over onto his back and fired a wild shot. Longarm felt the bullet whip-crack past his head as he unleashed a second shot that struck the man in the upper leg.

A moment later, Longarm slammed his boot down on the wounded man's thick wrist and put his pistol to the man's skull. "It's your choice," he said. "Give up or get dead."

The Taylor man had to think about that one for a second, and then he dropped his pistol and cursed at Longarm before fainting.

Longarm picked up the man's gun and checked his pulse to make sure that he wasn't going to get up and go anyplace. The pulse was little more than a flutter. Satisfied,

Longarm hurried to the gray gelding and galloped up the road after Cynthia.

He came upon the buckboard and the two women about a half mile up the road. Julia Konrad was stretched out and Cynthia was bent over her wetting a rag from her canteen.

Longarm jumped off the gray and hurried to them asking, "Is Julia all right?"

Cynthia didn't even look up at him. "She's alive. I haven't had time to see if she's really hurt or not."

Longarm glanced up, and saw the two horses pulling the buckboard filled with straw were standing with their heads low and their sides heaving. Off on one side of the road was a steep drop. If the buckboard had gone over that edge, Longarm figured that it, Julia, and the wagon horses would have all been destroyed.

"Cynthia," he said, letting out a sigh of relief, "I expect that you've saved Miss Konrad's life."

"And I expect I'll come to regret that, Marshal. Did you kill Rafe and Gaspar?"

"One is dead and the other is knocking on hell's door."

"I hope for your sake that they're *both* dead," Cynthia told him, finally looking up. "The Taylor men make terrible enemies and we're both their enemies now."

"I don't know if the second man I shot will live or not."

Cynthia stood up. "You take care of this rich bitch and I'll go see if the second one is alive or dead."

Something in her face told Longarm that Cynthia had it in her mind to finish off the second Taylor man if he wasn't already dead.

"That's not a good idea," he told her. "Just stay here with me and Julia. We can go back to check those two in a few minutes. Right now, Miss Konrad is the most important one."

"Not to me she isn't," Cynthia assured him.

Longarm thumbed one of Julia's eyelids up and he felt the pulse at her throat. He also saw that her hands and ankles were tied. He used his knife to cut her bonds, and then he stood up and said to Cynthia, "I'd have to arrest you for murder if you finished off that second Taylor man."

"You would?" Cynthia toed the dirt with irritation. "Marshal, don't you understand that if that man lives, he will make sure you and I are repaid in *blood?*"

"Maybe."

"No maybe about it!"

"Even so," Longarm argued. "You can't just be an executioner. I won't stand for it. It's against the oath I took as a lawman to take another man's life unless there is no other choice."

"Then the oath you took was stupid in this case."

"Cynthia," Longarm said, "please just do as I say. I need your help. We're still going down to Pine Valley."

"If we go there with a half-dead Taylor man, we won't be going to Pine Valley, Marshal. Instead, we'll be going into pine *boxes*."

Longarm knew that Cynthia was probably right. But that didn't change the fact that he wore a badge and had to uphold the law.

Chapter 14

Julia awoke thrashing and moaning. "Easy," Longarm said, trying to calm the dazed woman while she regained her mental faculties. "It's over. You're safe now."

The woman looked up at Longarm, and then turned to see Cynthia. "What is she . . . what . . ."

Longarm was quick to explain. "The two men who abducted you are shot and lying up the road. Cynthia was able to chase down the runaway buckboard before it flipped or went over the mountainside. There isn't a doubt in my mind that she saved your life."

"Thank you for that," Julia whispered, avoiding exchanging glances with Cynthia.

"Think nothing of it, ma'am," said Cynthia. "You've got a pretty good bump on the forehead, and I expect that you've got some bumps and scrapes that we can't see. But you're gonna be fine now."

"I'll repay you."

"I don't need or want any of your money," Cynthia said, anger flaring in her voice. "But it would help if you got on the first train back East where you belong and let the marshal and me try to find Bradford."

"I can't do that."

"Then you'll most likely get us *all* killed," Cynthia said harshly a moment before she turned and went to tend to the horses.

"She doesn't like me, does she," Julia said to Longarm. "What have I done that is so terrible to cause that much hatred?"

"I don't think she hates you," Longarm said, not quite believing his own assessment. "But she doesn't think you ought to be out here looking for Bradford. She sees you as a major problem."

"She's her own problem, Custis. But what is more important is why those two men abducted me."

Longarm shrugged. "They knew from the newspapers that you have a wealthy family and friends, so I expect they had some vague, half-baked plan to hold you for ransom."

"Where were they taking me?"

"Maybe to Pine Valley, but maybe not."

"Are they dead?"

"Probably."

"Good," Julia said forcefully. "They were both mean and I felt sure that they would kill me if I didn't escape. And once I almost did, when I managed to roll off the back of that buckboard. But because my hands and feet were bound, I landed right on my forehead and was knocked out cold."

"You could have easily broken your neck," Longarm told her.

"I know that. Please help me to my feet. I feel sick and need to stand and walk."

Longarm helped Julia up, and supported her as she took a few tentative steps. But Julia was very unsteady, and he knew that she would collapse if he let her go.

"You're not up to it yet," he said. "We can put you back in the wagon and you can rest and recover."

"Where are we going now?"

"To Pine Valley. I should deliver the bodies of those men to their family."

"After you shot them?" Julia shook her head. "I'm still a little dazed, but even so, I can't imagine that bringing those men back to their families is a very wise or healthy thing to do."

"Perhaps not, but it's the right thing to do. I'll tell their families the truth and that I ordered them to surrender, but that they refused and gave me no choice but to open fire."

Longarm helped Julia back into the wagon saying, "Just lie back in the straw and rest."

"I really don't want to lie in the straw anymore."

"Do it anyway," Longarm told her.

Cynthia came riding back up the road. "The second one bled to death," she told Longarm. "He had two bullet holes in him and leaked out."

Longarm looked up at her and saw not a shred of sympathy or regret. "You didn't try to stop the bleeding."

"Nope," Cynthia replied. "Gaspar was already dead and Rafe was no damn good. When I was young he chased me down to the creek and tried to . . . you know. But one of my brothers caught and beat him half to death. Rafe never forgave my brother and vowed to kill him sooner or later. Now, I guess that won't ever happen, so I'm happy."

"We'll load them up into the wagon and take them to their families in Pine Valley."

Cynthia's eyebrows shot up in disbelief. "The hell you say! We'll bury them in shallow graves up in the trees and not say a word to the Taylor family."

"Cynthia, I can't . . ."

Her eyes were like bullets and they pierced him. "Marshal Long, if you bring those bodies back to Pine Valley and the Taylor people find out that I was with you when this happened, it will not only come down on you, but also my family. We'll be dragged into this range war and I'll lose more than a few of my kinfolk to ambushers. I can't let you do that."

Longarm gave her words consideration while she added, "Dead is dead and them boys more than deserved what they got."

"All right," he finally agreed. "We'll bury them in the trees in unmarked graves. But don't be surprised if they're found and it all comes back upon us in spades."

"I'll take that chance," Cynthia told him.

"Okay then," Longarm said, "let's get it done and then let's get on down to Pine Valley."

It was dark when they finished burying Rafe and Gaspar Taylor up in the trees and under some heavy rocks so that the varmints couldn't dig up their corpses.

"How far to a settlement or town where we can put up in a little hotel for tonight?" Longarm asked when the burying was done.

"There's a farmhouse about five miles down the road," Cynthia replied. "I know the people there and they'll put us up for tonight. Grain the horses and won't charge us too much money."

"Good," Longarm said.

"What about that rich bitch?"

"What about her?"

"Marshal, you're ordering her to go back to wherever she came from, aren't you?"

"I can't order Miss Konrad to do a damn thing. She is insisting on traveling with us down to Pine Valley and she won't give up until she finds Bradford."

"She's worse than a fool. She's a dangerous fool."

"Cut her some slack, Cynthia. She's got more sand than you think."

"She'll get us *both* killed before this is done."

Longarm slapped the dirt from his palms. "Maybe so, but she's coming and you'll either have to get used to that notion, or you can leave us and return to your ranch."

"I'm your only hope to survive down south and you'd be fool enough to send me off?"

"I'd have no choice. My mind is made up, Cynthia, so you just have to make up your mind."

She expelled a deep breath of exasperation. "There is just one thing that I can't figure out."

"And that is?"

"How you've managed to stay alive so long as a lawman."

"Sometimes," Longarm admitted, "I've asked myself that very same question."

"I'll just bet you have."

They hiked out of the trees and down to the buckboard and horses. Julia had used the time to find a little spring and wash her face. She looked much better and completely alert. "What's the plan?"

"Cynthia says that there is a farmhouse just a few miles south that will take us in for the night."

"Rent me a real bed?"

"That's right," Cynthia said, with a little smile tight on her lips. "The marshal and I will sleep in the barn together on some straw."

"You can have him and the damned straw," Julia told her as she turned away.

Longarm gritted his teeth in anger. As if trying to settle a range war and find Bradford Gumm wasn't enough of a challenge, now he had to take responsibility for two women who hated each other.

Life wasn't fair most of the time, but a man just had to soldier along and do the best that he could in this troublesome world.

Chapter 15

Longarm awoke the next morning to the sound of a rooster crowing loudly not ten feet away. He and Cynthia had indeed spent the night sleeping in the back of the buckboard filled with straw. It wasn't a great situation, but Longarm had slept in plenty of worse places and when Cynthia had tickled his pickle, Longarm had found himself desiring her. He'd had to be careful not to rub the insides of his poor legs too hard against her, but that had not proved to be an impediment to their lovemaking. It was, Longarm thought, a damned good thing that the insides of her thighs weren't in as bad a condition as his own or there might have been a problem.

"What time is it?" he asked as he rolled out of the buckboard's bed, dusting off straw, and eyed the noisy rooster. "The sun is already high."

"Probably about nine o'clock. It was nice of that rooster to allow us to sleep in."

Longarm pulled on his pants, boots, and then reached for his gun. "How long will it take us to arrive in Pine Valley?"

"We should be there by nightfall, if we get moving and

121

stay moving. But I wouldn't recommend us going there directly. I think we'd be a whole lot smarter to go to my ranch and then go into town the next day with all my brothers and family surrounding us."

"Why is that?"

"Because the Taylor men would instantly recognize this buckboard and team of horses. Believe me, Custis, that bunch would shoot first and ask questions later."

Longarm supposed this was true enough. "All right. We'll go to your ranch and then I'll go into Pine Valley the next day. I've got to find out if anyone has seen Bradford or has any idea of where he went."

"Most likely he's dead, unless he really did head for the Apache country and didn't turn back."

"I've never been around the Apache all that much, but I do know they're tough fighters," Longarm admitted. "Did you say that you can make sign language with 'em?"

"That's right. And my family has always treated them fairly. In hard times we'll cut out a steer or two so they don't starve. We don't mind them using our grass or water so long as they don't tear up our fences and steal our horses. If you treat the Apache right, they'll treat you right. They're a fierce but honorable people."

"There are plenty who would disagree about being honorable."

"Ignorance is no excuse for the way we've treated them," Cynthia said defensively. "For years they have been shot on sight by both our soldiers and the Mexican soldiers as well."

"I'm sure that's true," Longarm said. "But we can talk about the Apache later. Right now I think I'd better get moving."

Longarm didn't bother to shave or even comb his hair. When he went to the door of the farmhouse, everyone was awake and had already eaten a hearty breakfast.

"You sleep in kinda late," the farmer, whose name was Ballard, observed. "I had expected to see you up and moving long before sunup. But then I guess you got busy, huh?"

When he said that he glanced at Cynthia, who was watering their horses at the well. Longarm knew what the old farmer was thinking and didn't give him any satisfaction.

"I'll have some breakfast now, if it isn't all gone."

"And that woman out there?"

"She will have some too."

Longarm saw Julia in the front room reading something and nodded to her, but she chose to ignore him.

Thirty minutes later and in grim silence, they hitched the team back up to the buckboard. Longarm tied the gray gelding to the tailgate of the wagon and Julia sat beside him on the seat. Cynthia elected to ride her mare.

"Comin' back through?" the farmer called as they headed out his yard.

"I hope so," Longarm called back, "but I couldn't tell you exactly when."

"If you're going to flash your badge around Pine Valley, you won't be coming back," the farmer warned as he headed out to his small field of corn and hay.

Around noon they saw a big flock of sheep being tended by two men and four dogs. The sheep were peacefully grazing on a hillside and the men were on foot.

"It's Hugh and Bill Condon, who are brothers," Cynthia informed Longarm as she drew her horse closer. "Damn the luck!"

"Why is that?" Longarm asked.

"Because they might recognize this team of horses and buckboard as belonging to the Taylor family. If they do, you can be sure they'll ask how we came to be using them. If they think we're in tight with the Taylors, they might even decide to try and ambush us a few miles down the road."

"Maybe they won't recognize anything," Longarm said hopefully.

"I wouldn't count on that," Cynthia said. "They aren't packing all that iron because they think it looks good on 'em or they're worried about coyotes killin' their sheep."

The Condon brothers were nondescript men who wore clodhopper boots and baggy pants and frayed blue shirts. Their hair was long and their faces were dirty like their hands. Longarm could smell them from a distance, and he could see that both were skinny, with sharp faces and prominent jaws and noses.

"They remind me a lot of the simple backwoods people in West Virginia I knew as a boy," Longarm observed. "Hard people who asked no quarter nor gave any."

"That pretty much describes them," Cynthia agreed. "They have always reminded me of the coyotes they hate so much. The Condon men are lean and cunning and every last one of them is a marksman."

Julia Konrad sat up straighter, aware that both men were staring at her with admiring and hungry eyes. "Marshal, I hope they're not going to cause us any trouble."

"I'll make sure that they don't," Longarm told her reassuringly. "Just be quiet and let me do the talking."

Julia glared at Longarm, then pursed her lips together tightly.

The Condon brothers came to a stop about twenty feet

directly in front of the buckboard. They nodded to Cynthia, and the taller of the two spit a stream of brown tobacco and drawled, "Afternoon, Miss Cindy. Who are your friends and where are you headin'?"

Longarm didn't like being ignored, and he jumped right into the conversation uninvited. "I'm United States Deputy Marshal Custis Long from Denver and this is our friend, Miss Julia Konrad. She is looking for her fiancé, Mr. Bradford Gumm, who I understand was here for a while and then disappeared. What can you tell me about him?"

"Don't know nothin' about that fella, Marshal." The taller one turned to his brother and said, "Billy, do you know what happened to that fancy lawman was hereabouts some months ago?"

"I sure don't."

Hugh Condon looked back at Julia and he smiled showing yellow, crooked teeth. "You're a real pretty one, miss. Would you like to come and join us for supper? We're havin' some mutton stew and maybe a little whiskey. Be a fun time for you."

"No, thanks," she replied, paling slightly.

"Maybe another time then," Hugh Condon said with a wink at his brother that caused the shorter man to giggle childishly.

"So," Longarm said, knowing how uncomfortable Julia was feeling, "you men have no knowledge of the whereabouts of Bradford Gumm?"

"I didn't even know he was missing," Hugh Condon said, trying his best to look even stupider than he probably was.

"Me, neither," Billy Condon added. "But I seem to recall seeing that buckboard and those two horses that's pullin' it. Don't they look familiar to you, brother?"

"Indeed they do," Hugh Condon said, his rifle resting in the crook of his arm. "I seem to remember they belonged to that dirty bunch of back-shooters called the Taylors."

"Yeah," Billy said, nodding his sharply pointed chin with a little bit of hair on the end. "Hugh, I do believe that is where I saw these horses and that worthless old buckboard."

"So, Marshal Long," Hugh said in a tight voice as he shifted his rifle so that it pointed more toward Longarm. "Are we wrong?"

Longarm knew that the worst thing he could do was to try to lie to these men, so he replied, "It did belong to the Taylors. But Miss Konrad is not a horsewoman so we got it from them."

"Did you pay 'em much money fer it?" Billy asked.

"They got everything they deserved," Cynthia told him. "Now you boys will have to excuse us because we have come all the way from Flagstaff and need to get to my ranch before dark."

The Condon brothers were burning with curiosity and wanted to ask more questions, but Longarm slapped the lines against the rumps of the horses and they almost ran the sheepherders down as they lurched forward.

"You people are in too damn much of a hurry!" Billy Condon angrily shouted as they passed. "Nearly ran us both over just now and that ain't neighborly. Miss Cindy, you shouldn't be hangin' around strangers that want to come down here askin' questions."

"I choose my own friends according to my best judgment, Billy," she shouted while riding past them. "That's why I've never chosen any of you Condons or Taylors as friends."

"That's not a nice thing to say to your best neighbors!"

Hugh Condon yelled. "We never caused your family no grief. You'd be makin' a big mistake to side against us with strangers."

Cynthia reined her buckskin mare around and stared at them for a moment, and then said through clenched teeth, "I'm not siding with anyone, Hugh. The marshal and the woman are here to find out what happened to Mr. Gumm. If you can't or won't tell us anything, then we have no talking to do."

Hugh Condon spit on the ground and hitched up his sagging britches. "You're actin' kinda high-and-mighty, Miss Cindy. You'd best be careful what airs you put on among us mountain people."

"Don't threaten her," Longarm ordered, pulling up the wagon and twisting around in his seat.

The Condon men shouted something else, but by then Longarm had put the team in motion and their words were drowned out by the creaking of the old wagon and plodding hoofbeats of the horses.

Longarm drove the buckboard about another mile and when he knew they were out of sight of the Condon men, he reined the team up and beckoned Cynthia over to talk.

"What do you think?" he asked the horsewoman.

"I think we've stirred up a hornet's nest," she replied. "They aren't quite as dumb as they look, and they sure didn't have any trouble recognizing the buckboard and Taylor horses. The question I'm wondering is if they believed your story about how we got them."

"They're hard, hard men."

"Just like the two Taylor boys you shot to death, only shorter and skinnier," Cynthia said from atop the buckskin.

"Let's keep moving. I don't want them to catch us camping on this road at night."

Longarm agreed, and forced the horses to hurry along.

They traveled steadily late into the afternoon before they come to fenced land. "This marks the north boundary of our family's ranch," Cynthia announced as she dismounted and opened the gate. "The ranch house is about two more miles up the road."

"Big ranch," Longarm said.

"In this country it takes a lot of land to make a decent living raising cattle and horses. Marshal, this isn't tall-grass country like you have way up north."

Longarm nodded with understanding. Up in Montana or Wyoming a few hundred acres of grassland might support a lot of cattle, but not down in the Southwest, where it took thousands of acres because the grass was so sparse and it could be miles between water holes.

"Cynthia, what is your family going to do when we get there and they find out that I've already caused you trouble with the Taylors and Condons?"

She considered the question for a moment, then said, "They won't be happy, but they won't shoot you . . . I don't think."

It was meant to be a joke, but the humor fell flat. Longarm glanced sideways at Julia, who had said barely a word the entire day. And as he drove the buckboard up the rutted ranch road, he wondered if she was finally coming to the conclusion that she'd made one hell of a big mistake leaving the East and all her rich and pampered high-society friends.

Chapter 16

Cynthia's ranch house was a big, two-story log cabin, and Longarm soon learned that her father had suffered a mild stroke and that her three brothers were all tall, handsome cowboys who didn't have a lot to say other than to talk cattle, weather, and horses.

Late that evening, when Longarm and Cynthia were alone sitting in front of a roaring fire, she told him, "My mother died when I was young and Father had his stroke about five years ago. He's still mentally sharp, but he has a hard time because he can't ride a horse or work cattle anymore except from the top of a wagon. He can't talk well anymore, but he never talked much anyway."

"Your brothers are still very respectful of him," Longarm said. "You can see it in the way they listen to him."

"Oh, yes," Cynthia said. "Father is a pioneer. He was a friend of Sam Houston and a Texan before he married my mother and came to Arizona. He very nearly chose to stay at the Alamo with Crockett and Jim Bowie. He would have stayed if he'd known what was going to happen to them all. But he had a brother in Arizona who was shot in a gunfight a few weeks earlier, so Father came here to help him recover and get back on his feet. The brother died of his bullet wounds and Father stayed on, and then found this country he wanted to ranch."

"So, if he had stayed in Texas, you'd have never been born and raised on this Arizona cattle ranch."

"That's right." Cynthia gave him a whimsical smile. "Isn't it funny how odd little circumstances change your life and the life of generations to follow? I've often thought that life isn't really what we plan it out to be . . . but it's what we make of what unexpectedly happens."

"I'd agree with that," Longarm told her.

Cynthia took his hand. "Take you and me, for example. If it wasn't for Bradford, whom I thought I loved and would marry, we would never have met and made love."

Longarm glanced around to make sure that this intimate conversation was not being overheard. He had a feeling that Cynthia's family was protective of her and would not look kindly on their lovemaking.

"And now we're sitting here in front of this big old fire in the middle of a mess that even you probably underestimate," she said.

"I'm not naïve about range wars or killing," Longarm said. "You saw what I did to Gaspar and Rafe Taylor. I've killed a lot of men and it's not something I talk about, much less brag about."

"I know that." She stared into the flames, and the colors that played across her pretty face and hair were spellbinding. "But what I'm getting at is that you plan to find Bradford Gumm and put an end to this feud between the Taylors and the Condons."

"That's right."

"But that might not exactly happen," she said, turning to look into his eyes. "You might find that nothing will stop the killing here until all sides of the fight are dead. And you might find out that Bradford Gumm is dead. Maybe you'll find his body, but probably not."

"If you're saying I could fail," Longarm replied, "I agree. And I have failed plenty of times in my life, so I won't be crushed."

"I'm glad to hear that because I think you *will* fail . . . and not because you're not capable, brave, and smart. But because some things just won't be fixed."

"We'll see," Longarm said quietly.

"And the other thing I wanted to get across is this thing of how life takes unexpected turns almost constantly. So what you are planning to do might turn out to be something altogether different."

"Cynthia," he said, stifling a yawn, "you're starting to talk in riddles. What is it that you are *really* trying to tell me?"

"I'm trying to tell you that you ought to keep yourself open to the idea that it might be your destiny to stay here in Pine Valley, then get married and to have children with me."

Longarm was suddenly wide awake. "Cynthia, listen, I think a great deal of you, but . . ."

She placed her fingertips over his lips. "Don't say any more. Just think about what I've told you and keep an open mind for possibilities that you never would have considered had you not come to this ranch."

"I'll never be a rancher or cowboy." Longarm put his arm across her strong shoulders. "I'm not cut out for living way out here in the wilderness chasing cows. I'd never be half as good at it as your father was or your brothers are."

"Maybe I don't want to stay here ranching all my life either," she said, surprising him. "I haven't hardly been anywhere except Flagstaff. I'd like to see some big cities and exciting places. Sometimes I feel . . . well, trapped. Suffo-cated and boxed in."

"Then you should go traveling."

"By myself? I'd be every bit as out of place in a city as Julia Konrad is in big country. I'm not a fearful person, but I think that being in a big city alone would be frightening."

"It can be a lot more dangerous than being in open spaces," he admitted.

"If we survive the feud and the Apache and Miss Kon-rad, could I go back to Denver with you . . . even if it is only for a short while? I'd always feel safe with you any-where we might go."

"Sure. I'll take you to Denver, if your family doesn't kill me at the mere suggestion."

"You might have hit on something there," she con-fessed. "My brothers can't cook for beans, and Father . . ."

Cynthia's voice trailed off, and Longarm understood how hard it would be to leave her father now that he wasn't completely capable. Longarm kissed her cheek. "I'm going to bed right now. It's much too late to be talk-ing so seriously."

"Life *is* serious."

"I know that," he told her. "And I'm going to bed to get some sleep."

She grabbed his wrist for a moment. "I could sneak down the hallway and . . ."

"No," he said firmly, but with a smile. "I've got enough trouble on my hands without making your family my ene-mies. So you stay in your bed and I'll stay in mine."

"All right," she reluctantly agreed. "But don't you dare let that rich bitch come creepin' around to your bed to-night. You couldn't hide it from me. I'd take one look at your face and know."

"Not a chance that will happen," he promised. "Right now she has decided she pretty much hates me."

"I hope she keeps thinking that way," Cynthia said.

Longarm got up and started to go to bed. But he turned to look at Cynthia still sitting on the hearth with her face aglow. "I'll want to ride into Pine Valley alone tomorrow morning."

"We don't always get what we want in life, Marshal."

He almost laughed. Would have laughed had the matter not been so deadly serious.

"We'll all ride into town together in the morning," Cynthia said. "We need supplies, so it's normal for us."

"*All* of you?"

"All except Father, who stays and guards the house."

Longarm didn't quite know what to say, so he just nodded. He had a feeling in his bones that this family wasn't going to let him ride into town alone no matter what he did or said to the contrary.

"Custis?"

"Yeah?"

"It would be best if that woman stayed here with my father tomorrow. She's got a big mouth and she'll only make things harder in Pine Valley."

"I agree."

"Good," Cynthia said. "Then *you* be the one to tell her she has to stay with Father."

"Julia may not be willing to do that."

Cynthia grinned. "Then she'll have to walk the seven miles into Pine Valley, and I doubt that she's up to the task."

Longarm nodded. "I think you're right."

"Good night."

Longarm had a stab of regret that they weren't sleeping

133

together in the straw in the buckboard and having themselves a great, passionate bout of lovemaking under the stars. But Cynthia was absolutely right . . . you didn't always get what you wanted in life.

Chapter 17

Julia Konrad was livid with anger. "Marshal Long, if you think you and the cowgirl are going to ride into Pine Valley without me, then you've got another think coming!"

Longarm stood his ground in the face of her fury. "I need to go into town and talk to the people about Bradford without you messing things up. Also, there might be trouble the minute I arrive wearing a badge, so it would be safer for you to stay here with Mr. Holden."

"I didn't come all the way down into this godforsaken country to play it safe!"

Longarm folded his arms across his chest to keep from strangling this woman. "Julia, you can't come along and that's final."

"You can't stop me!"

Longarm glanced over at Cynthia's father, who was sitting in a rocking chair on the porch. "You take care of her, sir. Don't let her try to hitch up that buckboard or saddle one of your horses."

The old man's left arm dangled loosely at his side, but his rugged face was uncompromising and he just raised a cattle whip in response. When Julia saw it, she paled slightly and then went stomping back to her room.

"So long, Daddy," Cynthia said, mounting her buckskin and joining Longarm and her three brothers, who were all heavily armed. "And don't you fret any about us. We're not any part of this range war and we won't let anything change that."

He nodded in solemn agreement.

Longarm had let it be known that he preferred not to have to ride the gray gelding, so the Holden men had given him a sorrel gelding.

"Let's go," he said.

They rode fast, alternating between the gallop and the trot, and so were able to come to the outskirts of Pine Valley in less than an hour. By then their horses were breathing hard and exhaling small clouds of steam in the cold mountain air.

"How do you want to play this, Marshal?" one of the Holden brothers asked when they reined up and gazed down at the little settlement located in a small, tree-ringed valley. Longarm could see the main street and the dozen or so single-story buildings. He could also see what appeared to be a couple of sawmills to the south.

Longarm thought a moment. "What are the chances that either the Taylor men or the Condon men will be in town today?"

"I'd say the chances are good that *both* families will be there. It's Sunday and the Condons go to the United Brethren Church and the Taylor families go to the Holy Gospel Church."

"Those families go to church and then bushwhack each other?" Longarm asked in amazement.

Cynthia understood the irony and said, "Their preachers

made each clan swear on the Holy Bible that there would be no blood shed between the two families on the Sabbath. But the other six days are open for hunting men."

"Astonishing," Longarm said, looking at his watch and noting it was almost ten o'clock. He was about to say something when the bells from both churches began to ring as if they were shouting in angry competition. "Let's go," Longarm said. "We can be waiting for them when they come out of church feeling good and godly."

"Those two families never feel godly," Cynthia told him. "But maybe they are a little less inclined to raise hell on Sunday."

So they rode down into the scenic little valley and then turned up the main street until they came to the general store, whose sign said it would not open until after church and then would close again at noon.

They tied their horses, and Longarm noted that the town's only two saloons were already open and doing business. The tall and grim-faced Holden brothers showed them no interest, which Longarm thought was a testament to their excellent judgment given the danger and circumstances.

"Custis, what are you going to do now?" Julia asked.

Longarm frowned. "I had lost track of the days and didn't realize that this was Sunday. I was hoping to just go around and ask some of the citizens about Bradford Gumm."

"I doubt that they'd have told you anything," Cynthia replied. "Everyone here would know he was a lawman and getting involved with his disappearance might get them into hot water . . . or worse."

"And why would that be the case?"

"It just would," Cynthia insisted. "There has been so much bloodshed and murder in this county that everyone is afraid to open their mouths for fear that they might say something that would make them an enemy of one feuding clan or the other."

Longarm saw an older couple walking up the street arm in arm. They were well dressed and looked intelligent, so he hurried across the street and intercepted them. "Excuse me," he said, "but may I ask you a question or two?"

Neither one of them was a bit pleased at his interruption, and the man said, "We were on our way to breakfast, sir."

"I'm United States Deputy Marshal Custis Long from Denver, Colorado, and I've come all the way over here to try and find Marshal Bradford Gumm and to—"

"We don't know a thing about the man," the woman said quickly as she tried to step around Longarm.

"Hold on a moment, please," Longarm ordered, moving to block their escape. "Whatever you tell me would be strictly confidential. And surely you must have seen Marshal Gumm and know that he's now missing. I'm just here to find the man, that's all. I really could use your help."

"We don't know where he went," the older man said, nervously glancing toward the United Brethren Church. "And we don't care. Marshal Gumm came here telling everyone that he was going to save them from any more killing. But then he clearly took the side of the Taylor clan, and that just made him an enemy of the Condon clan. Next thing we know, Gumm is riding with the Taylors against the sheep people and there was blood on his hands."

Longarm didn't believe it. "Are you saying that Marshal Gumm *killed* some of the Condon men during raids?"

"If he didn't kill them, then he was still part of those that did," the woman said, biting her lower lip with anxiety.

"So when the Condon men went after your friend, Marshal Gumm got scared. Last thing I heard, he was hiding. After that, we didn't hear another word about him and I say good riddance!"

"Mister, we really need to get some breakfast," the man said, sweating even though it was cold. "Would you please excuse us and don't you repeat what we told you or it will come back on us."

"I won't repeat anything I hear. But I have one more question and it's a quick one."

"All right then," the older man said, clearly upset because he kept glancing at one church and then the other. "What is it?"

"Have you heard any loose talk that Marshal Gumm was murdered?"

"Of course he was!" the man said in a hushed voice. "The Condons have bragged about it in the saloons!"

"It could be just loose talk."

"Marshal, it might be brag, that's true. But the Condons were after him and that I know to be a fact. And once that bunch of bushwhackers set their sights on a man . . . well, he had better have written out his will because he's already as good as dead."

The couple hurried up the street and disappeared into a small café.

Longarm went back to Cynthia. "They believe that the Condons murdered Bradford."

"Of course they would. They hate the Taylor clan and do a lot of feed business with the Condons."

"Even so," Longarm answered, "I felt like that couple was telling the truth."

"They were scared nearly witless."

Longarm saw a liveryman leading a mule out of a barn and into a round pine-pole corral. "I'm going to see what that man has to tell me."

Cynthia glanced at her brothers, who shrugged their broad shoulders and remained silent. Then she turned back to Longarm. "That's old man Purvis Alt. He won't tell you anything, so you'll be wasting your time."

"Maybe so," Longarm stubbornly replied, "but I'm going to ask the man anyway."

He waited until Alt had turned the mule into the corral and latched the gate, then said, "Sir, I'm a lawman from Denver and I'd like to ask you a question or two about Marshal Bradford Gumm."

"Don't know a thing about him," Alt snapped with irritation. "And I ain't got time to talk this morning. Got too many damn animals to feed and stalls to muck out. I sure as hell shouldn't have to work on Sunday, but the livestock I own and board still shit seven days a week."

"It'll just take a moment," Longarm said firmly.

Purvis Alt sighed. "All right, young man. What can I tell you?"

"What happed to Marshal Gumm?"

"I don't know."

"You've no idea?"

"Nope. But he's probably dead somewhere out in the woods."

"Have you heard anyone say that they shot him?"

"Nope. But Marshal Gumm was a lawman and we don't like the law in Pine Valley."

"Yeah," Longarm said, "so I've heard. There is a feud here that has claimed dozens of lives, and I'd think that you people would appreciate the law coming in and putting a stop to it."

Purvis Alt stared hard at him and hissed, "Both damned churches are gonna get out in a little while."

"I know that."

"Well, then, Marshal, you ought to know that when the Condons and the Taylors learn that you're here nosing around askin' all kinds of questions and botherin' old men like me, they're going to want to kill you like they did the other lawman with a big mouth and empty brag."

"I don't brag and I don't scare," Longarm said tightly. "And I'll be waiting when church lets out to speak to *both* sides."

The liveryman spit in the dirt between them. "That'll be good news to Woody Woodrow."

"Who is he?" Longarm asked.

"Our damned undertaker."

Purvis turned and went back into his barn without another word, leaving Longarm to shake his head at the ignorance of some backcountry people.

"Purvis didn't tell you anything, did he," Cynthia said.

"No."

"So what are you going to do now?"

"I'm going into the saloons and ask the same questions," Longarm replied. "I've learned that most men who drink on Sunday morning aren't afraid of dying."

"I'd never thought of that. Custis, we're going over to the cemetery to visit our mother's grave for a little while," Cynthia told him. "That's where we'll be waiting if you need us before church lets out. After that we'll go to the general store and buy some coffee, beans, and other supplies to take back to the ranch."

Longarm nodded with understanding and headed for the nearest saloon. He didn't think he was going to get any

141

more information from the drinkers than he had from the older couple or the crusty liveryman, but he'd come a long, long way to get to the bottom of Bradford Gumm's disappearance and he just wasn't going to leave a stone unturned in his search for some honest answers.

Chapter 18

Cynthia had been right about the Sunday morning. In fact, Longarm felt a whole lot of hostility when he entered both saloons.

The second saloon's bartender, however, did lean forward and whisper, "If I were you, Marshal, I'd head south looking for that big-talkin' Gumm fella. Last time I saw him, he was drunk as a loon and swearing that he was going to capture Geronimo . . . even though Geronimo has already been captured by the Army, sent to a damned reservation."

"Do you think that Marshal Gumm ever made it alive out of these parts?" Longarm asked quietly.

"I think it's entirely possible," the bartender said under his breath while pretending to polish some beer glasses. "The Taylors were guarding him like hawks, and probably escorted him into the next county before the Condon men ventilated his gizzard."

"Who would have taken him south? Which one of the Taylors?"

"I have no idea," the bartender said, abruptly ending the

conversation. "Would you like a drink? Just two bits, and the whiskey I serve is better than you'd expect to find in this one-holed-crapper town."

"No, thanks," Longarm replied.

"Marshal, don't come back soon," the bartender called out loud enough for everyone in the saloon to overhear. "Just get out of Pine Valley while you still can!"

Longarm turned at the door and surveyed the tough crowd. "Does anyone here know what *really* happened to Marshal Bradford Gumm?"

Not one man spoke up. Several spit into the sawdust at their feet and the rest turned back to their drinks, shunning Longarm and his question.

"I ought to let this town self-destruct," Longarm said to none of them in particular and at the same time each and every one of them.

Longarm slammed through the swinging doors and headed outside for some badly needed fresh air. He had never seen such an unfriendly and uncooperative bunch of Sunday saloon rats.

Longarm waited until he heard the bells ringing again and saw the quiet congregations exiting both churches at the opposite ends of the little Arizona town. Then he headed for the Holy Gospel Church, where the cattlemen were standing. He wasn't sure what he would say to the Taylors, but he knew he wouldn't beat around the bush and instead would confront them head-on.

"Good morning, everyone!" he called while still a short distance from the front of the white church and its milling dozen or so people. "My name is Deputy Marshal Custis Long and I need to ask you some questions about Marshal Bradford G. Gumm."

Like quicksilver coming out of a crucible, the Taylor

men left their women and streamed toward Longarm in a tight, angry group.

"Marshal Long, we just heard that you've got one of our buckboards and two of our good team horses," the oldest, largest man in the family shouted with a finger pointing at Longarm's chest.

Longarm stopped in his tracks wishing that he had a double-barreled shotgun clenched in his fists because that was the only thing that might bring this bunch of killers up short.

"I do have your horses and wagon," he admitted, planting his feet wide apart and dropping his hand toward his gun.

"We want 'em back and we damn sure want to know where Gaspar and Rafe are to be found!"

Longarm had two simple choices. He could tell this big, angry cattleman that he'd shot and killed Rafe and Gaspar in self-defense . . . which would surely result in his own death. Or he could lie and live a little longer to fight when the odds were remotely survivable.

Longarm chose to lie.

"I had to arrest them for tearing up a . . . a saloon. They're both safe but sorry resting in Flagstaff's jail."

"You *arrested* them?"

"That's right. However, just to show that I have no ill feelings toward your family, I brought your horses and buckboard back to Pine Valley. You can have them anytime."

The Taylor men stared at Longarm with hard, suspicious eyes. There wasn't a godly glance among them, and Longarm doubted if even his inspired, unrehearsed lie was going to keep him from dying on the spot.

"Hey, Quint, look at who's here! It's Miss Cynthia and her three see-nothin'-and-say-nothin' brothers," one of them said to their clan's leader.

Out of the corner of his eye, Longarm saw Cynthia and the Holden men hurrying toward him. He felt a flood of relief, but also shame because he had gotten them into this deadly game that couldn't be won.

"Marshal Long, is there a problem?" Cynthia asked, her own hand close to the butt of the Colt that rested on her shapely hip. "Or are you just passing along a Christian Sunday morning greeting?"

Before Longarm could answer, Quint said, "The marshal just told us that he arrested Gaspar and Rafe and threw them in the Flagstaff jail and that's why he's got our buckboard and horses."

"Well, wasn't bringing them back a neighborly thing to do?" Cynthia asked with a frozen smile on her lips.

The Taylor men were caught in a quandary. They couldn't seem to decide if Longarm and Cynthia were pulling their legs to save their hides or telling the honest truth.

Finally, Quint said, "Miss Holden, we'll be by your ranch house first thing tomorrow morning to collect that buckboard and our team of horses. And nothin' bad better have happened to them boys of ours in the Flagstaff jail."

"They'll be joining you in a few days," Longarm said, hating the lie, but determined that it would avoid a Sunday morning bloodbath.

"Good," Quint growled.

Longarm smiled. "Now that we've got that cleared up, I was wondering what you could tell me about Marshal Bradford Gumm. I understand that he was your friend."

"He wasn't *my* friend," Quint said, curling his lip. "But Miss Cynthia sure did like his flavor."

Cynthia blushed, but wisely kept quiet.

Longarm continued his questioning, although he knew

146

that the smarter thing would be to walk away while everything was still under control. "So you didn't protect him from the Condon men and take Mr. Gumm south where he'd be safe?"

Quint had started to turn to his men and say something, but now he stopped and changed his mind. "Marshal Long? Was that what you just told me that your name is?"

"That's right."

Quint pointed at him with his big finger. "Well, Marshal Long, I suggest you get out of town while you're still able and take these Holden people with you before I lose my temper and decide to go against the solemn promise I made to Preacher Smith and take *all* of your lives."

Longarm believed that he'd pushed this as far as it would go without a fight, so he said, "Nice to meet you men. Good to see you are all going to Sunday services so you can hope to save your souls."

Quint Taylor didn't seem to appreciate that snide remark, but he chose to let it pass and turned to the surviving men in his family. "Let's leave the ignorant to themselves and be at peace today as we promised on the Holy Sabbath."

But then one of the Taylor men shouted and pointed, "Look! The Condon boys are comin' up the street!"

Longarm and Cynthia whirled and saw the Condon men all heavily armed marching up the main street with blood in their eyes and grim, determined expressions on their thin, ferocious faces.

"Holy cow!" Longarm breathed, knowing that the two sides were going to finally settle this feud once and for all and Sunday promises to their preachers be damned. "There's about to be a war!"

Longarm grabbed Cynthia and propelled her out of the path of the two opposing clans. Cynthia's brothers were right behind them, and they all dove in behind a wagon as both sides pulled iron and hurled loud, vile curses.

"Custis, please don't even think of trying to stop this!" Cynthia cried, hugging Longarm and turning with pleading eyes to her three brothers. "You'll only get yourselves killed!"

"Good advice," Longarm said just an instant before the first Condon man threw up his pistol and opened fire causing all hell to break loose on Pine Valley's little main street.

Chapter 19

Longarm had sworn to uphold the law . . . always. Yet, as he crouched behind a wagon for protection, something inside of him just wouldn't let him stay out of a fight. He peered over the top of the wagon and watched men shooting down men. The two sides were both supposed to be expert marksmen, but stray bullets were flying in every direction, some shattering the windows of businesses.

"You stinking sheep-humpers!" Quint Taylor shrieked at the Condons as he emptied his pistol and took two bullets in the body. He folded at the waist, and a moment later Longarm saw the top of the man's head disappear, thanks to a sheep man's scattergun.

The two sides were mowing each other down in a bloody carnage while screaming oaths at the top of their voices. Longarm had been in the Civil War and had fought more than his share of terrible battles, yet he'd never seen more hatred between two sides than what he was witnessing now.

The last Condon man appeared to be mortally wounded, but was still standing and out of bullets. Longarm watched as the sheep man desperately attempted to reload his revolver with bloody hands that didn't seem to want to cooperate. All the Taylor men were down except Quint, who was covered with blood and staggering toward his last remaining enemy with cold fury in his demented eyes.

Longarm stood up and shouted, "Enough!"

But the two men had no intention of leaving even one of their sworn enemies alive, and so they closed on each other drawing long knives, and each sank their blades to the hilt in the other's body.

"Oh, my Gawd!" Cynthia whispered, her face pale with shock as the two men collapsed writhing and cursing in the dirt.

Longarm hurried to their sides just in time to hear their last crazed curses.

"It's over," Longarm announced to Cynthia and her brothers, who stared with nearly disbelieving eyes. "They're *all* dead."

"It's almost as if they had to kill each other to the last man standing," Cynthia said quietly. "And now the only ones left of their families are their women and children."

"Will *they* carry on this feud?" Longarm asked, wondering if the women and children were as obsessed with hatred as their men had been.

"I don't know," she confessed. "But I doubt it. The last thing the Condon and Taylor women will want is for their fatherless children to end up consumed by hatred and dying young."

Longarm was relieved to hear that. He surveyed the bodies, counting nine, and from the looks of them not one had died of a single gunshot. "It'll be a hard day for the town's undertaker."

"This feud was the only thing keeping him in business,"

Cynthia said. "He'll bury all of them, pocket a lot of cash, then leave this town never to look back."

"What will happen to Pine Valley now that this feud is finally over?" Longarm asked.

Cynthia thought about that a moment, then glanced at her three solemn brothers. When they didn't offer an opinion, she said, "I think that new people will start coming here and some that left afraid for their lives will return. It might take a few years, but I believe that Pine Valley will come alive again and be just as it was before the feud started."

"I think she's right," one of the brothers said. "We're about the only ones that were able to stay neutral, and that was tough. Anyone that seemed to take one side or the other of the feud had to leave their houses and flee for their lives in the night."

"It'll be like a rebirth," another of the brothers added. "This thing went on for way too many years. It's time for healing in Pine Valley."

Longarm agreed. "I should have tried to stop it, yet I knew that I couldn't. I might have broken this fight up . . . but given the way they hated each other, it would have only postponed an inevitable showdown."

Longarm saw people begin to filter out onto the main street in silence, and he turned to Cynthia. "I guess everything will change around here."

"Yes," she replied, "and very much for the better. But even years from now . . . generations from now . . . we'll be known as the town where too many foolish men died."

She looked off to the mountains. "So, Custis, what happens now?"

"When I left Denver, I was given two jobs to do in Arizona. One was to end this bloody range war . . . and it ended by itself. And the second was to find out what happened to Bradford G. Gumm."

"Can't he wait a few days?"

"I'm afraid not. I'll need to track him down and I'm not even sure where to start."

"I'll help you find him."

Longarm gave Cynthia a tight smile. "Maybe you ought to stay here and help with the healing."

"My family doesn't need healing," she answered. "And besides that, I also want to find Bradford. But what about Julia Konrad?"

"What about her?"

"She won't go back where she came from, and I wouldn't wish that woman on my family while we're off hunting for Bradford."

Longarm removed his snuff-brown Stetson and ran his fingers through his long, thick hair. "I sure don't want her to come along with us. Too hard and dangerous."

But Cynthia had another take on the situation. "Julia is absolutely certain that Bradford loves her, but the only one that man really loves is himself. And Bradford will never be satisfied until he either dies in a blaze of glory or becomes the man he thinks his father intended him to be."

"Do you still think he rode south into the Apache country?" Longarm asked.

"I'd bet my life on it."

"From what I've heard," Longarm told her, "that might be exactly what we will be doing when we go down there."

"Most of the Apache are on the reservations."

"But not all of them," Longarm said. "There are still renegades who would love nothing more than to kill me and capture two beautiful white women for slaves."

Cynthia smiled. "You just called me beautiful. That's the first compliment you've ever given me, Custis."

"Sorry about that. There is no denying that you are beautiful and so is Julia. That's why I . . ."

"Stop worrying, Marshal. Julia and I are going with you to find Bradford, and whatever happens to us is our own responsibility."

"And mine."

"Perhaps so," Cynthia conceded, "but you can't stop us, so get past that and we'll all do our best. I think that Bradford is dead, so we'll really be looking for his grave down in southern Arizona."

Longarm had been coming to the same conclusion, but he hadn't wanted to tell that to either woman. And there was nothing that brought worse luck than tracking a dead man's trail.

Chapter 20

When Longarm, Cynthia, and her brothers returned to the Holden Ranch late that afternoon, Mr. Holden was sitting alone on the porch with a crooked smile on his rugged face.

"They killed each other off, didn't they," he said, knowing the deadly outcome as sure as if he'd actually been in Pine Valley that bloody Sunday.

"Yes they did, Father," Cynthia replied. "Quint Taylor and Patrick Condon were the last two standing. When they ran out of bullets, they knifed each other to death."

"They were hard, hard men," the rancher said.

Longarm nodded with agreement. "I've never seen any harder or more filled with hatred."

The old man rocked silently for a moment, then said, "We'll do what we can for their women and children. If they want to leave this country, we'll buy them out for a fair and honorable price."

"Where is Miss Konrad?" Longarm asked.

"Had to hog-tie her."

"You *what?*"

He rocked for a few more seconds while Longarm digested this information; then the rancher added, "The fool woman was determined to go after you even though I warned her to stay put. When she wouldn't, I knocked her over the head with a board and tied her up. Wasn't easy. She's stronger than I thought."

Cynthia leaned forward in her saddle. "Father, you clubbed Miss Julia Konrad with a board?"

"Yep. She gave me no choice."

"But . . ." Cynthia was flying out of the saddle and hurrying past her father into the house.

"Did you hit her hard?" Longarm asked, praying that the old man hadn't killed Julia and wouldn't need to die in prison or perhaps even face a hangman's rope.

"Naw," he said, rocking and grinning. "I just sort of stunned her a little. She started yelping her head off like she was a pig being stuck. After a time I got weary of that, so I stuffed a rag in her mouth. I think she's gone to sleep for a while."

Cynthia appeared a few moments later from the house leading an obviously dazed Julia Konrad. She helped the woman into a chair, and Julia turned her swollen, tear-streaked face to the old man and gave him the most awful look that Longarm had ever seen.

Longarm dismounted and tied his horse at the rail. "Julia, how is your head?"

"He tried to *kill* me, Marshal Long," she hissed. "I want you to arrest that old bastard and send him to prison!"

"I can't do that," Longarm told her. "I've got to go find your fiancé. Too bad that you're hurt and can't come along."

"I'm coming!"

"Then I guess you aren't hurt enough to file charges against Mr. Holden. 'Cause if you were to insist on doing that, you'd have to do it in Flagstaff. But Cynthia and I are heading south to find Bradford. So what is it to be? South with us . . . or north to Flagstaff?"

Julia swore passionately under her breath, and then turned on Mr. Holden to vow, "If I were a man I'd kill you right now!"

To which he replied, "Missy, if you were a man I'd have broken your skull with that board and the town's undertaker would have one more body to bury."

Longarm thought that Julia was going to go over the edge and attack the old rancher, so he stepped in between them saying, "We'll be riding out to find Bradford first thing tomorrow morning. I expect you'll be feeling much better by then, Julia."

In response, she climbed unsteadily to her feet and went to the door. Cynthia tried to help her but was rebuffed, and Julia raised a finger and pointed at all of them saying, "I know you think that I'm going to just forget what this man did to me today . . . but I won't. I'll get even after I find Bradford. And when I tell him how I was treated at this ranch, you all had better beware."

The door slammed shut and Julia was gone. Longarm heard a sound off to the side and when he turned, it was to see the disabled old Arizona rancher giggling.

Chapter 21

Almost a week later, Longarm, Cynthia, and Julia stopped their tired horses and gazed down on the dry and ugly border town of Naco. It wasn't much of a town, really, just a few dozen wood shacks in addition to some crumbling adobes. Around the little settlement burros grazed freely on prickly weeds while feral pigs rooted and quarreled in piles of rotting garbage.

"This is exactly the kind of place where Bradford would probably come if he were looking to meet the Apache," Cynthia told them. "I've never been here, but my father and oldest brother were one time when they came to buy horses and Mexican cattle. They bought livestock cheap, but they were all rustled on the way out and my family barely escaped with their lives."

"Why on earth would *anyone* come to such a squalid, ugly place?" Julia asked through lips cracked dry by the unrelenting Arizona sun. "Do we really have to go down there among those uncouth people?"

"We do if we want to keep hunting for your Bradford," Longarm told her. "But that much said, I'd much rather you two women stayed out here in the brush hidden from sight.

I've been to a number of border towns, and it's an experience you don't want to share."

"I'm not staying out here to wait," Cynthia told him. "I'm thirsty and hungry."

"So am I," Julia added. "Do you think that they'll have a clean bed to sleep in and decent food to eat in Naco?"

"Probably not," Longarm told her. "But if you both insist on coming into town with me, then we stay close together. There are always slave traders operating in these border towns and you would both be a highly valuable prize."

Julia didn't understand. "What do you mean 'slave traders'?"

"I mean that these people will steal women from wherever they can and take them deep into Mexico where they are auctioned or sold to the highest bidder. That might be a rich Mexican landlord who fancies a young white woman, or it might be a renegade Apache leader who wants to implant his seed in a white woman so that she will bear his child."

"No," Julia breathed.

"Yes," Longarm said. "And any child born of a slave would also be considered a slave and not treated as well as a stray mongrel on the street."

Julia swallowed hard. "Isn't there any law along this border?"

"Some," Longarm replied. "But the Arizona Rangers can't patrol the entire border and they're not sanctioned to go into Mexico. So if you are kidnapped, you're pretty much lost, never to be found."

"Would Bradford become a slave?" Cynthia asked.

"I doubt it," Longarm answered. "A white man would be tortured or maybe sent to a silver mine where he'd be worked to death. If his captor was smart, a white captive might be ransomed for whatever money could be gotten from his relatives. Usually, though, he'd be killed outright."

"Maybe Bradford is right down there in Naco," Cynthia said, excitement rising in her voice. "If he is, we can get him to come back with us and get out of this awful country in a few hours."

"Maybe," Longarm answered, "but I have my doubts. Still, there's only one way to find out and that's to ride down there and start looking for Bradford."

"Then let's stop talking and go," Julia said irritably. "At least we can find some food and refreshments."

Longarm nodded in agreement. As a United States marshal he was not supposed to go into Mexico, and he hoped that he would not have to do so. If he crossed the border, the *federales* would not respect his badge or authority. Most likely the opposite would be the case and he would be treated badly . . . perhaps even beaten, humiliated, and made an example of.

"Let's ride," he said, "but my advice to you women is to pull your hat brims low and try to look like men."

"That could never happen with me," Julia said, clearly insulted. "But Cynthia looks and acts like a common cowboy."

"Oh, shut up!" Cynthia warned. "Or I'll knock you off that horse into a cactus and you'll be picking thorns out of your high-and-mighty ass for the next week!"

Cynthia looked ready to carry out her threat, and Julia wisely clamped her jaw and said no more as they rode down through the cholla cactus into the shit-hole border town of Naco.

Longarm was aware of many eyes following them as they trotted up the littered, fly-infested street and brought their weary horses to a stop in front of a small café that advertised good food at low prices.

"Let's get something to eat right here," he told the women in a purposefully loud voice as he slipped his Winchester out of his saddle boot and gave a hard glare at the men who were nearest. "Just tie your horses up tight and we'll sit inside next to a window so that no one will dare to steal our horses or provisions. If they try it, I'll shoot them without a warning."

The café was dirty, with two old dogs in one corner and a mangy yellow cat sitting on the counter. Longarm took a table next to the front window not ten feet from their horses, and motioned for Julia and Cynthia to sit down across from him.

"What do you want to eat?" a big, unkempt man with a black beard demanded as he wiped his greasy hands on his dirty apron. "We got fried beans, beef, and pork. Sourdough bread and coffee. I can also bring you a bottle of whiskey or tequila because you don't want to drink the water."

Longarm looked to the women, who seemed unsure, so he said, "Bring us everything you mentioned except the tequila. Do you have any beer?"

"Yeah, but it's green and cloudy. It will get you drunk, but also sick as dogs."

"Then we'll drink whiskey providing it doesn't have anything floating around in the bottle."

"Nothing but a few dead flies," the man said, laughing because he thought that was a good joke and it had obviously shocked the two women.

"If I get the quick-step from your food," Longarm warned, pinning the man with a hard look, "I'm coming back and shitting on your floor. Then I'll shoot you down."

The big man's smile evaporated into a snarl. "Meals will cost you a dollar each."

Longarm knew that he was being robbed, but Julia was reaching for her money and saying, "Please cook everything very well."

"Sure thing, miss. I boil the meat until it falls off the bones, and then I fry it and spice it so that you can't taste what has gone rancid." He placed his hands on his hips and said, "Miss, you look like a lady that might have a sensitive stomach, so I'll give you a piece of good advice."

"And that is?"

"Stick with the bread, beans, and the whiskey."

"Thank you," Julia said, clearly intimidated by the man and the prospect of eating in such a dirty café.

When they were alone, Longarm pulled the rag aside that passed as a curtain. "Look at the attention we've created."

Indeed they had caused quite a stir in Naco. At least a dozen tough men, about half white and the rest either Mexican or Apache, had come to examine their horses and outfits.

"Maybe you ought to go out there and order them away," Julia nervously suggested. "Those are really terrible-looking men."

But Longarm shook his head. "They're not breaking any laws, but you two young women have really gotten their interest up."

"Do you think we're going to get out of Naco without serious trouble?" Cynthia asked, her hand brushing her holstered Colt.

"I think so," Longarm replied. "I'll go out and ask them if anyone has seen Bradford and tell them that I'm a United States marshal. Maybe that will backfire, but I doubt it. We are still in Arizona."

163

"Is there a river or something nearby that marks the boundary between the United States and Mexico?" Julia asked.

"Not in this part of the country. In fact, there probably isn't any border marker at all."

"Then how will we know if we have to cross the border?"

"Good question," Longarm said as the whiskey was brought to their table along with three stained and mismatched glasses.

"No worms or shit in that bottle of rotgut," the café owner said with clear amusement. "And just because you are such pretty ladies, I took it upon myself to strain out all the dead flies."

Julia gasped and looked ready to faint, but Cynthia just gave the man a go-to-hell look.

Longarm poured them each a half glass and held his own up to the window. "It's pretty clear so drink up, ladies. It might be a long, hard day in Naco."

"What are you three doing in a place like this?" the café owner asked, lingering close to their table.

"Looking for a man named Bradford Gumm. Do you know where we can find him?" Longarm asked.

"I should have known that people like you would be looking for a man like that. As a matter of fact, Mr. Gumm was in Naco."

"Was?" Julia demanded.

"That's right. He said he was a sworn lawman and that he wanted to meet Quantana."

"Who is that?" Cynthia asked.

"Haven't you heard of Quantana?" the man asked, looking shocked at her ignorance. "Why, he's the most famous renegade we have across our border. Quantana is one of the last of the great Apaches left still fighting the United States and the Mexican armies. His band probably doesn't number a dozen, and he'll disappear for months into the Sierra Madre of northern Mexico before he suddenly raids, rapes, and murders. No one knows where or when he'll attack next and he's about wiped out all the little ranchos in this part of Arizona."

"Why would Mr. Gumm be after such a man?" Longarm asked.

"Because Cochise and Geronimo ain't runnin' loose and doin' any damage anymore. Quantana is the last of his breed and he's building quite a reputation. Mr. Gumm told everyone that would listen . . . and we all would listen because he always bought us whiskey . . . that he'd become famous if he captured the last free Apache raisin' hell."

"Go on," Longarm ordered, sure that he was hearing the truth.

"Bring the food first," Cynthia said. "I'm famished."

"You do look a little on the skinny side," the café owner said. "Most of the women in Naco are fat Mexican whores. None of them could fit even one of their flabby legs into your sweet britches."

The man was leering down at Cynthia's lap, and Longarm reached out and grabbed his wrist, then twisted it hard while saying, "These are ladies so you'd better watch your manners, mister."

"This one ain't such a lady," the man said, pulling free and still leering at Cynthia. "But I'll grant that other one is."

"I'm engaged to marry Mr. Gumm," Julia said stiffly. "And that's why we've come all this way to find him."

"Well," the café owner said, "you'll just have to go a little farther, I'm afraid. But if I were you three, I'd take a strong notion to turn your horses around and ride north just as fast as they can run. This ain't good country for pretty women. Too many bad things happen to 'em."

"I'm a United States deputy marshal," Longarm said, showing the man his badge. "And I won't tolerate any lawlessness or bad behavior toward myself or these ladies."

"I hear you, Marshal. I'm a law-abiding man. But those outside?" The man's eyes slid through the window at the motley bunch collected near the hitching rail and horses. "Now they are entirely another matter. And you know what?"

"What?" Longarm asked.

"They don't give a damn about you being a federal lawman. 'Cause the only law in Naco and along this entire border is the law of the gun. And those boys out there will test you, Marshal. They'll test you with bullets and blades and they'll crap on that shiny badge when you're lyin' in the dirt bleeding to death and facing your Maker."

"Get the damn food," Longarm growled. "We aren't paying you three dollars to listen to your mouth."

"Sure thing, Marshal." He chuckled, but it had a definite evil and ominous sound. "But I think it's an even bet that you will be eatin' your last supper."

Chapter 22

"I hear that you three are in a big hurry to find Mr. Gumm," the half-breed said in a quiet undertone.

Longarm turned to see a man that looked as if he had been born and bred in hell. His face was pocked where his spotty black beard would not grow and his eyes were gray and close-set. A livid ridge of scar ran from one ear down across his mouth to his pointed chin. His right ear was partially missing, and he wore two guns, one on each of his narrow hips.

"That's right," Longarm replied, "and who are you?"

"Doesn't matter, Mr. Marshal. The only thing you need to know is that I know where you can find the soon-to-be-famous Bradford G. Gumm."

"Keep talking."

"He's with Quantana's band."

"I've already been told that," Longarm said, looking unimpressed. "Tell me something new."

"I can take you to Quantana and Gumm. Is that news worth payin' for?"

Longarm had judged this man at first sight and his judgment was far from favorable. If ever he'd seen a lying, low-down rat, this man surely fit the bill. "Where are they?"

"Not far across the border. One day of hard ridin'. Two days draggin' along those handsome women. But you'd never find Quantana and his men on your own. But they'd find and kill you."

"And you think that you can get us to Gumm without that happening?"

"I know I can. But it'll cost you plenty."

"How much?" Longarm asked.

"A thousand dollars for me and another thousand for Quantana." The man grinned. "And that will be *cash*."

"Too much."

The man shrugged, then turned to walk away saying over his shoulder, "That's just about what I expected you to say, Marshal. So I guess that you'll hang around Naco for a while until someone either shoots you dead or steals you blind. It's up to you and of no mind to me."

"Hold up there!"

The man turned around and there was a cruel half smile on his face.

"How do you know where Quantana's band is hiding and how can you be sure that Gumm is still alive?"

"I am Quantana's blood brother as anyone in town can tell you. I saved his hide a long time ago. Now you need to understand that we ain't chummy and I'd never drink with him, but Quantana owes me and an Apache always pays his debts."

Longarm still wasn't convinced. "And Bradford Gumm?"

"He's riding with Quantana. He wants to write that Apache's life story and go back East and make himself famous sellin' books and givin' lectures on the last of the fighting Indians. Gumm told me he figures to become famous that way."

Longarm was contemptuous. "Bradford Gumm is a fool if he thinks that he can make money off the misfortunes of the Apache. Besides, while everyone has heard of Cochise and Geronimo, no one outside of this part of Arizona has ever heard of Quantana."

"That will soon change."

Longarm's eyes narrowed. "What is that supposed to mean?"

"It means that Quantana is planning raids that will make those by Cochise and Geronimo look like Sunday picnics."

"And does Bradford Gumm expect to go along on these murderous rampages?"

"Beats me, Marshal. But I'd think you have to be there to see and write about it," the man said.

"What's your name?"

"Like I said, it don't matter."

"It does to me."

"All right. Call me Reed."

"I don't have two thousand dollars."

"Then we're both wasting our breath," Reed told him.

"However," Longarm quickly added, "Miss Konrad has some money and jewelry that is worth a small fortune."

"I don't want jewelry," Reed said, curling his lip.

"Then I'll ask her how much cash she can give you. As for Quantana, well, we'll just have to wait until we meet him to cross that bridge."

"If you meet Quantana, you'd better have something valuable he wants or he'll burn you alive."

"When could we leave to go to find them?"

"How long will it take for you and those women to saddle your horses?" Reed asked.

"I'll go talk to them and see what they think," Longarm told the man. "I'll meet you back here in less than an hour."

"Hump!" Reed snorted, looking completely disgusted. "I thought that you, being a big and important federal marshal, would be in charge. Looks like the women are wearin' your outfit's britches."

Longarm didn't like that remark even a little bit, yet he decided to let it pass. The important thing was finally catching up with Gumm and putting an end to this chase.

"Reed, before I go I want you to be real sure of something."

"And that is?"

"If you're leading us into a trap or taking us into Mexico and we don't find Gumm inside of three days," Longarm warned, "I'll kill you faster than you can blink an eye. Don't think that because I'm a marshal I'm going to try to arrest and then take you back to some judge . . . because I won't. If we cross the border, my oath and authority of office mean nothing."

"I'll take you to 'em, but I ain't gonna do it for free and Quantana ain't going to accept cheap jewelry. He'd rather hear you scream and watch you burn at a stake. And you know what he'll do to those pretty women."

Longarm didn't even want to think about it as he left the man and went to discuss this dangerous outing with Cynthia and Julia. When he told them about Reed, both wanted to accept the man's offer despite the dangers.

"Are you sure you know what we'll be getting into?" Longarm asked them both. "Because once we're in Mexico our lives are up for grabs."

"Did you believe the man really knows how to take us to Bradford?" Julia asked.

"Yes. And I let him know I'd kill him if he was taking us on a wild-goose chase."

"But he still wants to do it?"

"That's right," Longarm said, turning to Julia. "But he wants cash. So how much do you have?"

She didn't hesitate. "I have hidden three thousand dollars in my bags."

"Three thousand!" Longarm cried in amazement. "I told you not to bring much cash."

"I don't listen to you, Marshal. And isn't that turning out to be fortunate?"

"I guess so," Longarm said. "Three thousand ought to more than square it with Reed and Quantana."

"Then let's get Bradford out of Mexico and back where he belongs," Julia said, folding her arms across her chest and raising her chin defiantly.

Longarm turned to Cynthia. "You don't have to come with us . . . and you really shouldn't."

"'I sure as hell can't stay here in Naco, so I might as well take my chances with you.'"

"All right," Longarm said, "then let's buy some food and supplies and get ready to ride."

"We're leaving *today?*" Julia asked, looking shocked and upset.

"That's right. Or did you want to sleep in one of this town's cribs?"

"What's that?"

"It's a little place not much larger than a two-holer outhouse where the ladies of the night do business," Longarm told her. "Because that's the best you could do since I haven't seen even a run-down hotel in Naco."

"Then let's go," Julia said, her lower lip quivering.

"Let's just get this done so that Bradford and I can return to the East, get married, and look back on the West as nothing more than a passing nightmare."

Longarm headed to find Reed and make his deal. The half-breed would want some money in advance, but he'd let Julia wait to pay the man on their way out of Naco.

Chapter 23

"How much farther?" Longarm asked. "You said one or two days and this is the second day out from Naco. We haven't much water in the canteens and both the women and these horses are playing out."

"See those peaks?" Reed answered, raising his hand and pointing. "That's where Quantana is camped. Those are the Sierra Madres, and there are more caves and hiding places there than you could explore in a hundred years. Only the Apache know the hiding places and water holes. Even the *federales* won't go up into the mountains because they know they'll be trapped in some box canyon and wiped out in an ambush."

"Have you been up there before?"

"Yes," Reed said. "But not for many years. It wasn't until now that there was only one surviving renegade Apache band."

"Quantana's," Longarm said.

Reed nodded. "My guess is that he and his men have been watching us for the last day. When we start up into those mountains we'll be stopped, and that's when we're in the most danger."

"You mean they might shoot and ask questions later."

"That's exactly what I mean," Reed said, removing his bandanna and wiping sweat from his eyes. "This horse I'm riding is an Indian pony given to me by Chief Quantana. I'm betting that they'll recognize the horse even if they don't recognize me from a distance."

Longarm removed his hat and then shielded his eyes from the hot sun. They were low on water and his throat felt as if he'd swallowed a handful of hot sand. Their horses were suffering and the women, especially Julia, were at the end of their endurance. Today had to be the day they found Quantana's camp and Bradford Gumm.

Had to be.

They picked their way up an ancient Indian trail through mostly prickly pear and cholla cactus, although there were a few tall saguaros with their thick arms lifting toward the unrelenting sun. "There's a water hole just around that rock," Reed told them. "I hope it ain't gone dry."

It hadn't gone dry, and they rested and drank water until their bellies bulged and their horses seemed to take on new life. Then they tightened their cinches and continued up the mountainside.

"There they are!" Reed whispered, his voice stretched with tension. "They've purposely put themselves into our sight."

"That's good, I'd guess," Cynthia said, overhearing their half-breed guide.

"It's neither good nor bad," Reed replied. "And they're too far away for me to recognize Quantana. I'm not sure that I would anyway."

Longarm was taken aback by this candid admission. "What the hell is *that* supposed to mean!"

174

"It means that I haven't seen Quantana in over seven years."

Longarm ground his teeth in angry silence. He did not want to say anything more to frighten the women, who were already close to being terrified.

"Here they come," Reed said in a low, tense voice. "I'll do the talking. Marshal, you and the women stay back and wait."

"I can sign language with Apache," Cynthia told the man.

"Great," Reed replied without enthusiasm as he nudged his Indian pony ahead. "But you ought to know that Quantana speaks a little English. He don't do it much and tries to act like he doesn't understand, but he knows more than he ever lets on. So don't be fooled. The man is smart as a whip."

Longarm watched as Reed made his way forward up a narrow and winding path toward six Apache who were on foot and well armed. Longarm could see that they were very dark and short in stature, but tremendously broad in the chest and shoulders. When their half-breed guide neared the Apache, Longarm could faintly hear words being spoken. The conversation seemed strained and went on for almost fifteen minutes. At last Reed waved to Longarm and the two women indicating that they were to come on up and join this small band.

Up close the six renegade Apache were even more intimidating. They were a mix of boys in their teens and old men, but the one thing they had in common were their eyes, which were as cold and dark as agates.

"What are they saying?" Longarm asked.

"I told them that you are a United States marshal. They have never seen one down here this far into Mexico before and wonder if you are a friend of the *federales*. I told you you were not because they hate the *federales* and will kill them on sight."

"I don't even know a *federale*," Longarm said. "What about Bradford Gumm?"

"They say he is up at their camp with Quantana and the others. It is not far. Less than a mile off."

One of the fiercest-looking of the Apache moved over to Julia and stared straight up at her. Then, he reached out and stroked her thigh.

"Uh!" she cried, recoiling and reining her horse back from the man.

"Don't show fear!" Cynthia warned. "Don't show anything."

"But . . . but he's *touched* me. What if he . . ."

The Apache fighter saw and heard the fear in Julia and grinned, showing that he was missing most of his front uppers. Then he grunted something to the others in his band and they started up the mountainside in single file. They wore breechclouts and moccasins and bandoliers of bullets along with skin bags that sloshed with water. The sound of the water made Longarm even thirstier than he had been, and he hoped that there was more of it in the Apache camp and that he lived to slake his thirst.

The camp was a swirl of starving dogs and hard-faced humanity. Quantana's people numbered no more than two dozen and more than half of them were thin women and children. There were few men of fighting age other than the six that had intercepted them on the slopes down the mountainside. These people lived in wikiups made of brush and woven branches. Several gutted deer were hanging in mesquite trees along with a half-eaten burro coated with green blowflies.

"Oh, my God," Julia whispered, hand coming to her mouth. "I have never seen people so bad off. This is pathetic!"

"Be quiet," Cynthia warned. "They are proud and the very last thing they will ever accept from whites is pity."

Two men were sitting under a brush arbor and when they stepped out into the sunlight, Longarm knew at once that they were Quantana and Bradford Gumm. But Gumm didn't look anything like a white man now. His hair was long and tangled and he wore a full beard and animal skins just like the Apache renegades.

"Bradford? Bradford!" Julia cried, jumping off her horse and running across the camp scattering dogs to throw herself into her fiancé's arms. "Oh, Bradford, my darling! We've come to take you home!"

Longarm and Cynthia sat their horses as still as stone statues while Bradford Gumm's mouth dropped with astonishment. Then Gumm looked at Quantana and something passed between the two men that Longarm could not read. But he didn't have to read the message because Bradford Gumm tore Julia's arms away and pushed her away in disgust. When she threw herself at him again, he punched her in the face as hard as he might have hit any man.

Julia's head snapped back as she dropped, and it was clear to Longarm that the woman had been knocked out cold. He wanted to attack Gumm, but he knew that would be suicide given their situation in this Apache camp.

"What are you doing here!" Bradford shouted at them. "Are you people crazy! Cynthia, my God, have you lost your mind!"

Cynthia kicked her horse forward until it was no more than ten feet from Quantana and the former Eastern socialite. "Bradford, we've come all the way down here to take you back."

"But I don't have any intention of going back! I *chose* to

be here and fight beside these brave people. I am going to ride with Quantana and make *history!*"

Longarm knew it was time to speak up. "Mr. Gumm, I'm Marshal Custis Long and I was sent by powerful friends of yours to find and return you safely home."

Gumm now turned his wrath on Longarm. "You fool! You arrogant, ignorant fool! What kind of a man are you to bring two women like this to Quantana's camp?"

"They insisted. Once, they loved you." Longarm glanced at both women and added, "Maybe they still do."

"I don't care!" he screamed. "I am Apache now! Look at these people. They *need* me!"

For a moment not a word was spoken and not a sound was made, even from the quarreling, whining dogs. Then Quantana raised his fist and began to speak in his own tongue to their guide Reed. Longarm's eyes flicked from the half-breed to the renegade chief, back and forth, trying to decipher what was being said and knowing that his own fate and that of the two white women was being decided.

At last, Reed said in a trembling voice, "We'd better hand the cash over now or it looks like we're finished."

Julia had cash in her saddlebags, and Longarm dismounted and tore it loose, then extended it toward the Apache chief. Strangely, it was Bradford Gumm who snatched the money from Longarm's outstretched hand and then counted it with almost childlike excitement.

Gumm turned to Quantana and exclaimed, "Chief, there is almost two thousand dollars here! Enough for many more guns and ammunition. Enough for food and fresh horses to use on our raids."

"*You* are raiding with this bunch," Longarm heard himself say. "What the hell has gone wrong with your mind killing innocent people?"

Bradford Gumm was a big man, and he spun around and hit Longarm even harder than he'd struck Julia. Longarm staggered and nearly fell. Would have fallen had it not been for his horse and the saddle horn he grabbed for support.

"You ignorant fool!" Bradford shouted. "You bring these women here and now you question *my* behavior?"

Longarm wiped blood from his mouth and tongued a loose front tooth. He wanted in the worst way to wade into Bradford and beat him to his knees. But instead, he had to hold himself back.

Spitting blood, Longarm growled, "You've got money and now we want to leave this place in peace . . . with . . . or without you."

"You should never have come here," Gumm declared after saying a few words to Quantana in the Apache tongue. "I can't save you now. I can't save *any* of you."

"Now wait a minute," Reed said, jumping from his horse and running up to Quantana. "Chief, I saved your life. Remember? You *owe* me for that?"

In response, Quantana drew a large hunting knife from his belt and in one swift and unbroken moment he gutted the half-breed from belly to brisket. Reed lifted onto his toes and then he spit in the Apache's face with the last burst of his breath. Quantana yanked out his knife and sliced Reed's throat open as he was falling.

Longarm could feel the sweat breaking out across his body, and when he looked at Gumm the man was almost smiling.

"Gumm, you've lost your mind and your soul. You've gone crazy with the same blood lust as Quantana and you'll go to hell with the vultures picking out your eyes."

"You're a dead man talking," Gumm replied quietly.

"What you say means nothing to me, but I am sorry for these women."

"Then let them go," Longarm asked, trying to keep the pleading out of his voice. "If you let me take them back across the border unharmed, I'll promise you . . ." And then the magic word came to his lips. "I'll promise you *fame*."

"What?" Bradford was suddenly all interest.

Seeing this, Longarm pushed on quickly. "Without witnesses you'll just die a nobody. But if we are spared and allowed to return safely, then we'll tell your story."

"But you won't tell the truth," Gumm said after a moment of reflection. "You'll tell the world that I've joined a desperate band of Apache raiders. But look around you, Marshal. What do you see? Starving people. Hopeless people trying to avoid being herded onto a reservation where they would be treated worse than dogs."

Cynthia interrupted. "Bradford, we'll tell everyone including the press about the women and children that we see here and of their terrible suffering and hardships."

"But will you tell them about *me?*" Bradford yelled, wildly pounding his chest with fists and greenbacks. "Will you really tell them about me trying to help these dirty, ignorant savages!"

Something changed in Quantana's expression at those words and he turned to Gumm with his knife still dripping Reed's warm blood. And then, then he said in perfect English, "Dirty, ignorant savages?"

Too late did Bradford Gumm realize his mistake in speaking his honest mind. Too late did he throw up his hands and start to beg for understanding and forgiveness from the "dirty, ignorant savage" that he had supposedly befriended.

Again Quantana's hunting knife flashed at the exposed throat, and again the torrent of warm blood cascaded forward. Bradford staggered and tried to close the gaping wound, but another Apache yelped and jumped onto his back with his knife working the kidneys and close in between the ribs.

As Bradford went down thrashing in death, the Apache hacked off his nose and his ears.

Cynthia, despite her tough ranch upbringing, swayed in the saddle and then began to vomit.

Longarm drew his six-gun and pointed it at Quantana expecting to be instantly riddled by bullets and arrows. "United States marshal," he said, "no *federale*. No *federale!*"

For a moment his fate and those of Julia and Cynthia hung suspended like a feather caught in the breeze, and then Quantana looked down at Reed and Bradford Gumm still spilling their life's blood into the dirt and said, "Marshal—go."

"Not alone. I'm taking the women."

Quantana reached down and extracted the thick wad of money still clutched in Bradford's dead hand. He counted it out slowly, his lips silent but moving. When he finished, he nodded as if he had reached some inner agreement before he looked at the three white people and at the gun in Longarm's fist pointed at his heart.

"Chief, I'm not handing over this gun. If I die now, then you'll go with me."

Quantana touched his own chest and then he made an odd sign. Longarm didn't take his eyes off the man. "Cynthia, what does he want?"

"Your badge. He wants your marshal's tin star."

Longarm had never given his up badge to anyone. It was against all that he stood for . . . but far more importantly, it could be *replaced*.

So without taking his gun off the Apache renegade chief, Longarm used his left hand to slowly remove his badge from his vest pocket. It was quite an impressive badge and it would cost him five silver dollars to replace back at the Denver office.

Quantana grinned and showed the badge to his followers, who whooped and howled with admiration. Then he pinned it on his breechclout and did a slow little dance to the delight of his laughing, clapping people.

"Go," Quantana said finally, stopping and turning back to Longarm.

And that was what Longarm did just as fast as he could scoop up the unconscious "rich bitch" and sling her across her saddle.

"Will they come after us?" Cynthia yelled as they trotted out of the squalid Apache camp.

"No," Longarm said. "Quantana saved face and got to keep my badge."

"Would you have actually shot him?"

"Why not?" Longarm replied as they hurried their horses down the steep trail. "I always vowed to go down fighting."

"You're *crazy!*"

"So was your Bradford Gumm!"

"Are you still going to take me with you to Denver!"

"Let's talk about it when we cross the border!"

It was nearly dark when they came down out of the barren Sierra Madres. They would stop for only minutes at the last water hole, and then ride all night pushing until they were back and safe in the United States.

Longarm fervently hoped that they would not run into a patrol of the *federales*. And he also really hoped that the Apache wouldn't suddenly decide to come after them. But

he was a man who had always survived by trusting his in-
stincts and gut feelings. And right now, they were telling
him that he and Julia were going to make it all the way to
Denver.

Watch for

**LONGARM AND THE
MIDNIGHT MISTRESS**

the 336th novel in the exciting LONGARM
series from Jove

Coming in November!

LONGARM

Explore the exciting Old West with one of the men who made it wild!

GIANT-SIZED ADVENTURE FROM
AVENGING ANGEL LONGARM.

Longarm and the
Undercover Mountie
0-515-14017-1

This all-new, giant-sized adventure in the popular all-action
series puts the "wild" back in the Wild West.

U.S. Marshal Custis Long and Royal Canadian Mountie
Sergeant Foster have an evil town to clean up—where
outlaws indulge their wicked ways. But first, they'll have to
stay ahead of the meanest vigilante committee anybody
ever ran from.

GIANT-SIZED ADVENTURE FROM AVENGING ANGEL LONGARM.

COMING IN NOVEMBER 2006...

LONGARM AND THE OUTLAW EMPRESS
0-515-14235-2

WHEN DEPUTY U.S. MARSHAL CUSTIS LONG STOPS A STAGECOACH ROBBERY, HE TRACKS THE BANDITS TO A TOWN CALLED ZAMORA. A HAVEN FOR THE LAWLESS, IT'S RULED BY ONE OF THE MOST ⊠POWERFUL, BRILLIANT, AND BEAUTIFUL WOMEN IN THE WEST...A WOMAN WHOM LONGARM WILL HAVE TO FACE, UP CLOSE AND PERSONAL.

AVAILABLE WHEREVER BOOKS ARE SOLD OR AT
PENGUIN.COM